ABT

D0312827

Christmas Stories
from the
South's Best Writers

Edited by Charline R. McCord
and Judy H. Tucker

Foreword by
Elizabeth Spencer

Illustrated by
Rick Anderson

PELICAN PUBLISHING COMPANY
Gretna 2008

Library of Congress Cataloging-in-Publication Data

Christmas stories from the South's best writers / edited by Charline R.
McCord and Judy H. Tucker ; foreword by Elizabeth Spencer ; illustrations
by Rick Anderson.
p. cm.
ISBN 978-1-58980-600-9 (hardcover : alk. paper) 1. Christmas stories,
American—Southern States. 2. Short stories, American—Southern States.
3. Christmas—Southern States—Fiction. 4. Southern States—Social life
and customs—Fiction. 5. Southern States—Fiction. I. McCord, Charline
R. II. Tucker, Judy H.
PS648.C45C4585 2008
813'.0108334—dc22

2008011742

Printed in China
Published by Pelican Publishing Company, Inc.
1000 Burmaster Street, Gretna, Louisiana 70053

CONTENTS

FOREWORD

Carrollton Christmas in Olden Days

Just when I as a child started thinking about Christmas each year, I can't say precisely, but soon after Thanksgiving, I would guess. It was a magical thought. I awaited the miracle with certainty, for the miracle would certainly come. I was a believer. I believed in everything: Santa Claus and the Easter Bunny went right along with the Apostles Creed and might as well have been included in it, though being Presbyterian we didn't often repeat the creed. Also, I once caught my mother dyeing Easter eggs and lost the bunny early on.

I was very easily scared. Thinking of Santa, I began to wonder if I would hear the reindeer hooves on the roof. It made me tremble to think that.

Each year my brother and I were sent out into the wooded pasture back of our house to pick out a Christmas tree. We would find a small cedar, with evenly grown branches, and tie a string around it for the handyman to come and cut it down. Brought in the house, set up as usual in the corner of the wide hallway, it looked a lot bigger, waiting for its trim. This was before the time of electric lights strung together and plugged in. The candles were wax, rather like those for birthday cake, and were set in small metal holders, each to be clamped to a tree branch. Then ropes of tinsel were swirled among the branches. We had a star! It was painted aluminum and glittered, and somebody got up on a ladder and fastened it to the very top branch. So there was the Bible story, all mixed in.

My mother kept an old sheet to spread around the base of the tree. There was something called "artificial snow," cotton with shiny flakes, to be scattered around, all ready for the presents to come and lie waiting, while we felt through the paper wrappings and tried to guess, though told not to.

But preparations at the house were small compared to those at the church. Every year my mother was in charge of the Christmas pageant. The Presbyterian pageant was the famous one, and the whole town would turn out for it. Many were actually in it.

We rehearsed every afternoon. The choir, the Bible readings, the setting made to look like a barn with piles of hay and stalls for cows and donkeys, and of course the manger, holding straw piled over a flashlight. Some pretty young woman from the church would be robed in blue to sit by the manger and wait for shepherds and wise men. They would come down the aisles in different lots, while music about them was lustily sung. The choir, far to the right of the scene, was hidden by draperies made of blankets and green boughs and plants. The best singers in town came to swell the music. The small space grew crowded, and once somebody fell out of the choir. It was later said that he was drunk.

I was usually an angel. My wings were attached by wire made from coat hangers. I wore a head band of tinsel, which scratched, and a white robe made from a sheet. Later when I grew several inches taller I was cast as a shepherd and wore a dingy bathrobe fastened with safety pins and carried a crook.

On Christmas Eve the church flamed with light. Presbyterian churches are usually plain. We had one or two stained-glass windows, mostly to commemorate former members who had died, but the lights provided on those evenings were centered around the stage. Where they were set up elsewhere I can't remember, only the impression of many lights. We had a small pump organ. The church was full. It was probably quite cold. No snow.

Two of my mother's elder brothers had gone into military service and so had been stationed in far-off places like China and the Philippines and had brought back as family gifts certain bronze table ornaments. These could be easily converted into vessels for gold, frankincense, and myrrh. I believe she found some way to light something like incense in one of these, but Presbyterians are not equipped with censers; we had swept all that out with the papacy. Yet I do think she managed it, along with so much else.

Oh, the music! It commenced softly from the organ before the singing, while everybody was settling into seats and getting quiet. Then, all of a sudden, we were the faithful, invited to come, joyful and triumphant. We were in Bethlehem! Somebody now began reading from the Bible, and the old story came alive again. Shepherds were coming in with one or two kids on all fours, covered with what looked like sheepskin. A big angel (my brother) appeared before them, waving a cardboard horn painted silver. Next all the little angels crowded 'round. Now, the lights were on Mary and her manger with the flashlight glowing under the straw.

The three kings were lined up outside in the vestibule and marched down the aisle to their special song. You could see their pants legs with cuffs sticking out beneath their robes, and you could recognize the good everyday faces of Sanders and Hansborough and Bennet fathers from under their cardboard crowns. But tonight they were kings from the Orient, bearing gifts.

The glowing evening was finally over. Whoever had fallen out of the choir had long been reinstated to sing "Silent Night" with all the rest.

My mother in utter exhaustion must have thanked the Lord that it all had gone off well for yet another year. When we reached home she went right to bed.

As for me, all this time, since right after Thanksgiving, I had been busy praying. I very much wanted a baby brother and thought if I asked God every night He would hear me and give me one. I specified: Let him be born on Christmas Day. My reasons for this desire were, I think, mainly centered in the brother I had. He was seven when I was born and must have thought some malevolent fate had wished this worrisome creature into his favored, pampered life. He had to share! He had to be nice! He had, at the very least, to put up with me! My prayers may have been heard but were not answered. God had put in place other arrangements for acquiring baby brothers.

On Christmas morning, waking was done to shouts of "Christmas gift!" The belief was that if you said it before the other person, he or she would owe you a gift. This foolishness went on through breakfast, every time anybody trailed into sight. But then, the tree. Gifts had by now accumulated to a good height on that snow-covered sheet. Somebody struck a match and lighted all the little candles while my mother hoped the house wouldn't catch fire. We called in the cook (Laura) and the handyman (Bill) and my father's foreman (Charles), all of whom had presents waiting. There followed a great swishing of paper, cries of delight—"Just what I wanted!" "How did you know!" "Just look!" "Oh, goody!"

In speaking of prayers for a baby brother, I now wonder what gift I might have prayed to have for Christmas. The truth is, I don't remember. My parents were generous to a fault; we had only to wish once, out loud, and they would remember and try to satisfy. I think once I got a bicycle, which I loved, rode, and fell off of regularly for years.

The other unanswered prayer was for snow. It seldom, if ever, came.

I stacked my presents carefully and took them to my room.

What else to tell? Christmas dinner? Yes, of course! Turkey, rice and gravy, candied sweet potatoes with marshmallows, English peas, some sort of salad—altogether more than any one human could get down. Ambrosia! My mother made it from fresh cocoanut broken open outdoors with a hatchet, drained, and grated, with fresh oranges, a cherry or two, and what else I forget, though certainly fruit cake.

Filled and groaning, some would go take naps. But some, I remember, on one warm Christmas afternoon went out into the yard and played ball with Bob, our collie dog. My brother or one of the cousins, who might have wandered by, would fling a tennis ball over the house. The house was one story, but the roof was high. Bob would be on the far side. He would catch the ball and come tearing around the corner with it. The game was now to catch Bob, who would pretend to be racing away with it, dodging and circling, but finally letting go, only to race back around the house, and the game would start again. It was such a warm day that the boys were sweating in rolled-up sleeves.

But that very Christmas night the wind groaned and rose. Freezing air swept in from the north, down the great continental basin of the Mississippi River, straight for us, way down in Carrollton. The thermometer went plunging into the 20s. Would the pipes burst, would we have no water?

Christmas was over, for another year.

In recalling these memories, some glow more than others. But one of them, living on, is my love of Christmas carols. Each time I hear "O Little Town of Bethlehem," I think of Carrollton and of little towns all over the world on Christmas Eve, and invariably I burst into tears.

Elizabeth Spencer

INTRODUCTION

What if there was no Christmas? No Christ in our lives? No fir tree trimmed to the max, no brightly wrapped packages, no gathering and giving, no gifts? What if there were no families feasting, no faith or forgiveness? What if there was no Bible? What if there were no books?

You can rest assured, we'd keep the stories alive, but we might not celebrate Christmas the same way, in all its meanings—both holy and secular—without the printed word. We'd tell and retell its story, as we do among family and friends gathered around the fireside, but a book that preserves the story—there is no substitution for a book.

There's a reason the invention of the Gutenberg press is considered one of the major events of history. The primitive instrument, fashioned after a wine press, could print about three hundred pages a day. The Gutenberg Bible is considered one of the most magnificent examples of the art of printing—yes, the *art* of printing.

Without the book, we probably would not have the good fortune to experience "The Christmas Monkey," Glen Allison's memorable story about three children making a magical Christmas out of heartbreak. We would not feel the cold and loneliness of "Christmas 1910" on a snowy Midwestern plain as only Robert Olen Butler can describe it. Can such a stark environment sustain tenderness, hope, and even love? In the skillful hands of Butler all things are possible.

Margaret McMullan would not be at the fireside with us to tell about a good-hearted handyman who hung "The Swing" and helped a lonely rich kid have "the best Christmas ever." We probably would not have the good fortune to share an evening with Suzanne Hudson and hear her story of a family shattered by tragedy, who with courage, and love, put it back together again.

We would miss the insightful story of a boy named "Luke" and an early morning hunting trip that Sheryl Cornett invites us on. Through her words, you can feel the moisture in the cold, icy morning air, see the bright stars gleaming in the night sky, anticipate the crackle of dried leaves underfoot, and maybe even pick up a whiff of wood smoke in the air. You can taste the sausage biscuits eaten in the cab of the truck and feel a tug at your heart as the man and the boy slowly begin to trust one another.

Only written words can do justice to the delicacy of Mary Ward Brown's description of "The Amaryllis." The life cycle of an amaryllis has lessons to teach, and Judge Manderville is an astute pupil. As the flower unfolds its beautiful petals, the judge's tight, lonely world expands. Yes, without the printed word, we would probably never meet Kay Sloan and hear her expansive tale of sly, knowing humor about aliens visiting the Gulf Coast and saving a marriage in "Occasion for Repentance."

What a shame it would be if we missed the telling of Mark Richard's "The Birds for Christmas." This is a tough story of boys in an orphanage facing a stark Christmas, but it is infused with humor and great charity. Without this book, we would never meet a lonely girl named Lavender Blue, a character Jacqueline Wheelock has drawn to perfection in "Blue's Christmas." Blue will delight you and surprise you. And remind you that miracles do still happen.

As much as we'd like, we'd probably not have Ruth Campbell Williams at the Christmas dinner table to tell the insightful story of "Queen Elizabeth Running Free." It's all about a strong woman claiming her strength and her future. Nor would we have the opportunity of sitting spellbound as Olympia Vernon weaves the mystical tale of "The Cold Giraffe." Vernon is a fresh, new face on the literary landscape, and she will be heard from again.

We live in a time of hurry and scurry, hustle and bustle. A time when cars are too slow, red lights are too long, and breakfast, lunch and dinner happen in the car while zipping from point A to point B. Reading is often relegated to down time, something we do while trapped in the doctor's waiting room, stuck in an airport terminal gate, or reclining at home in our sickbed. Many of us are watching in silent and helpless disbelief as time-honored newspapers across this country are dying a slow and painful death because the camera and the computer are faster and sexier than the printing press. Yet we remain a people of the printed word; we value the written record and cherish the legacy of stories. Imagine not being able to pen a Christmas letter to that special soldier in Iraq, to send your own Christmas story of hope from the relative safety of this country into the heart of darkness, chaos, and war. Words matter, stories matter, and books matter.

So, let's sing the old familiar carols, celebrate Christmas with church and family, and make a toast to the printing press, the book, and most of all the scribes who write them and the readers who take them into their hurried lives. There's an old saying: I am a part of all I have met. At the risk of being presumptuous, we would like to add a second chorus: All I have read is always a part of me. May we all give and receive good words, good stories, and good books this holiday season!

Merry Christmas to you all!

Charline R. McCord and Judy H. Tucker

Christmas Stories
from the
South's Best Writers

Christmas 1910

by Robert Olen Butler

Scenic, S. Dak.
Dec. 24, 1910

Mrs. Sadie Yinkey
R.R. #2
Edgar, Neb.

My dear gallie: Merry Christmas and Happy New Year. This [is] my barn. Am hugging my saddle horse. Best thing I have found in S.D. to hug. Am sending you a trifle with this. With love, Abba.

My third Christmas in the west river country came hard upon the summer drought of 1910, and Papa and my brothers had gone pretty grim, especially my brother Luther, who was a decade older than me and had his own adjacent homestead, to the east, that much closer to the Badlands. Luther had lost his youngest, my sweet little nephew Caleb, to a snakebite in August. We all knew the rattlers would come into your house. We women would hardly take a step without a hoe at hand for protection. But one of the snakes had got into the bedclothes and no one knew and Caleb took the bite and hardly cried at all before it was done. And then there was the problem with everybody's crops. Some worse than others. A few had done hardly ten bushels of corn for forty acres put out. We weren't quite that bad off, but it was bad nonetheless. Bad enough that I felt like a selfish girl to slip out of the presence of my kin whenever I had the chance and take up with Sam my saddle horse, go up on his back and ride off a ways from the things my mama and papa and brothers were working so hard to build, and I just let my Sam take me, let him follow his eyes and ears to whatever little thing interested him.

And out on my own I couldn't keep on being grim about the things that I should have. There was a whole other thing or two. Selfish things. Like how you can be a good daughter in a Sodbuster family with flesh and blood of your own living right there all around you, making a life together—think of the poor orphans of the world and the widows and all the lost people in the cities—how you can be a good daughter in such a cozy pile of kin and still feel so lonely. Mary Joseph and Jesus happy in a horse stall, forgive me. Of course, in that sweet little picture of the Holy Family, Mary had Joseph to be with her, not her brothers and parents with their faces set hard and snakes crawling in your door and hiding in your shoe.

So when the winter had first come in, there hadn't been any snow since the beginning of November and it was starting to feel like a drought all over again, though we were happy not to have to hunker down yet and wait out the dark season under all the snow. There was still plenty of wind, of course. Everybody in our part of South Dakota shouted at each other all the time because of the wind that galloped in across the flatland to the west and to the north with nothing to stop it but the buffalo grass and little bluestem and prairie sand reed, which is to say nothing at all. But the winter of 1910 commenced with the world dead dry and that's when he came, two days before Christmas, the young man on horseback.

We were all to Luther's place and after dinner we returned home and found the young man sitting at our oak table in what we called our parlor, the big main room of our soddy. He'd lit a candle. The table was one of the few pieces of house furniture we'd brought with us from Nebraska when Papa got our homestead. Right away my vanity was kicking up. I was glad this young man, who had a long, lank, handsome face, a little like Sam actually, had settled himself at our nicest household possession, which was this table. And I hoped he understood the meaning of the blue tarpaper on our walls. Most of the homesteaders used the thinner red tarpaper at three dollars a roll. Papa took the thick blue at six dollars, to make us something better. People in the west river country knew the meaning of that, but this young man had the air of coming from far off. We all left our houses unlocked for each other and for just such a wayfarer, so no one felt it odd in those days if you came home and found a stranger making himself comfortable.

He rose and held his hat down around his belt buckle and slowly rotated it in both hands and he apologized for lighting the candle but he didn't want to startle us coming in, and then he told us his name, which was John Marsh, and where he was from, which was Bardstown, Kentucky, county of Nelson—not far down the way from Nazareth, Kentucky, he said, smiling all around—and he wished us a Merry Christmas and hoped we wouldn't mind if he slept in the barn for the night and he'd be moving on in the morning. "I'm bound for Montana," he said, "to work a cattle ranch of a man I know there and to make my own fortune someday." With this last announcement he stopped turning his hat, so as to indicate how serious he was about his intentions. Sam's a dapple gray with a soft puff of dark hair between his ears, and the young man sort of had that too, a lock of which fell down on his forehead as he nodded once, sharply, to signify his determination.

My mama would hear nothing of this, the moving on in the morning part. "You're welcome to stay but it should be for more than a night," she said. "No man should be alone on Christmas if there's someone to spend it with." And with this, Mama shot Papa a look, and he knew to take it up.

"We can use a hand with some winter chores while we've got the chance," Papa said. "I can pay you in provisions for your trip."

John Marsh studied each of our faces, Mama and Papa and my other older brother Frank, just a year over me, standing by Papa's side as he always did, and my younger brother Ben, still a boy, really, though he was as tall as me already. And John Marsh looked me in the eye and I looked back at him and we neither of us turned away, and I thought to breathe into his nostrils, like you do to meet a new horse and show him you understand his ways, and it was this thought that made me lower my eyes from his at last.

"I might could stay a bit longer than the night," he said.

"Queer time to be making this trip anyway," my papa said, and I heard a little bit of suspicion, I think, creeping in, as he thought all this over a bit more.

"He can take me in now," John Marsh said. "And there was nothing for me anymore in Kentucky."

Which was more explanation than my father was owed, it seemed to me. Papa eased up saying, "Sometimes it just comes the moment to leave."

"Yessir." And John Marsh started turning his hat again.

Mama touched my arm and said, low, "Abigail, you curry the horses tonight before we retire."

This was instead of the early morning, when I was usually up before anyone, and she called me by my whole name and not Abba, so it was to be the barn for John Marsh.

Papa took off at a conversational trot, complaining about the drought and the soil and the wind and the hot and the cold and the varmints and all, pretty much life in South Dakota in general, though that's the life he'd brought us all to without anyone forcing us to leave Nebraska, a thing he didn't point out. He was, however, making sure to say that he held three hundred twenty acres now and his eldest son a hundred sixty more and that's pretty good for a man what never went to school, his daughter being plenty educated for all of them and she even going around teaching homesteader kids who couldn't or wouldn't go to the one-room school down at Scenic. John Marsh wasn't looking at me anymore, though I fancied it was something he was struggling to control, which he proved by not even glancing at me when Papa talked of my schooling, in spite of it being natural for him to turn his face to me for that. Instead, when the subject of me came up, his Adam's apple started bobbing, like he was swallowing hard, over and over.

I slipped out of the house at that point, while Papa continued on. I walked across the hard ground toward the little barn we kept for the saddle horses, Sam and Papa's Scout and Dixie. When Papa's voice finally faded away behind me, I stopped and just stood for a moment and looked up at the stars. It's true that along with the wind and the snakes and the lightning storms and all, South Dakota had the most stars in the sky of anywhere, and the brightest, and I had a tune take up in my head. *I wonder as I wander out under the sky. . . .* Christmas was nearly upon us and I shivered standing there, not from the cold, though the wind was whipping at me pretty good, but because I realized that nothing special was going on inside me over Christmas, a time which had always all my life thrilled me. Luther had even put up a wild plum tree off his land in a bucket of dirt and we'd lit candles on it, just this very night. And all I could do was sit aside a ways and nod and smile when anyone's attention turned to me, but all the while I was feeling nothing much but how I was as distant from this scene as one of those stars outside. And even now the only quick thing in me was the thought of some young man who'd just up and walked in our door, some stranger who maybe was a varmint himself or a scuffler or a drunkard or a fool. I didn't know anything about him, but I was out under this terrible big sky and wishing he was beside me, his hat still in his hands, and saying how he'd been inside thinking about only me for all this time. *How Jesus the Savior did come for to die, For poor ornery people like you and I.* Ornery was right.

I went on into the barn and lit a kerosene lamp and Sam was lying there, stirred from his sleep by my coming to him at an odd time. His head rose up and he looked over his shoulder at me and he nickered soft and I came and knelt by him and put my arm around his neck. He turned his head a little and offered me his ear and waited for my sweet talk. "Hello, my Sammy," I said to him, low. "I'm sorry to disturb your sleep. Were you dreaming? I bet you were dreaming of you and me riding out along the coulee like today. Did we find some wonderful thing, like buffalo grass flowering in December?"

He puffed a bit and I leaned into him. "I dream of you, too," I said. "You're my affinity, Sammy." Like John Marsh not looking my way when Papa spoke of me, I was making a gesture that was the opposite of what I was feeling. My mind was still on this young man in the house. I suddenly felt ashamed, playing my Sam off of this stranger. In fact, I was hoping that this John Marsh might be my affinity, the boy I'd fit alongside of. I put my other arm around Sam, held him tight. After a moment he gently pulled away and laid his head down. So I got the currycomb and began to brush out the day's sweat and the wind spew and stall-floor muck and I sang a little to him while I did. "When Mary birthed Jesus 'twas in a cow's stall, With wise men and farmers and horses and all," me putting the horses in for Sammy's sake, though I'm sure there were horses around the baby Jesus, even if the stories didn't say so. The stories always made it mules, but the horses were there. The Wise Men came on horses. There was quite a crowd around the baby, if you think about it. But when he grew up, even though he gathered the twelve around him, and some others too, like his mama and the Mary who'd been a wicked girl, he was still lonely. You can tell. He was as distant from them as the stars in the sky.

So I finished up with Sam and then with Scout, and Dixie had stood up for me to comb her and I was just working on her hindquarters when I heard voices outside in the wind and then Papa and John Marsh came into the barn, stamping around. I didn't say anything but moved behind Dixie, to listen.

And then Papa said, "I'm sorry there's no place in the house for a young man to stay."

"This is fine," John Marsh said. "I like to keep to myself."

There was a silence for a moment, like Papa was thinking about this, and I thought about it as well. Not thought about it, exactly, but sort of felt a little wind gust of something for this John Marsh and I wasn't quite sure what. I wanted to keep to myself too, but only so I could moon around about not keeping to myself. John Marsh seemed overly content. I leaned into Dixie.

"I was your age once," my papa said.

"I'll manage out here fine."

"Night then," Papa said, and I expected him to call for me to go on in the house with him, but he didn't say anything and I realized he'd gone out of the barn not even thinking about me being there. Which is why I'd sort of hid behind Dixie, but he'd even ignored my lamp and so I was surprised to find myself alone in the barn with John Marsh. I held my breath and didn't move.

"Hey there, Gray," John Marsh said, and I knew he was talking to Sam. "You don't mind some company, do you? That's a fella."

I heard Sam blow a bit, giving John Marsh his breath to read. It was not going to be simple about this boy. Him talking to my sweet, gray man all familiar, even touching him now, I realized—I could sense him stroking Sam—all this made me go a little weak-kneed, like it was me he was talking to and putting his hand on. It was like I was up on Sam right now and he was being part of me and I was being part of him. But then I stiffened all of a sudden, got a little heated up about this stranger talking to my Sam like the two of them already had a bond that I never knew about. I was jealous. And I was on the mash. Both at once. In short, I was a country fool, and Dixie knew it because she rustled her rump and made me pull back from her. She also drew John Marsh's attention and he said, "Hello?"

"Hello," I said, seeing as there was no other way out. I took to brushing Dixie pretty heavy with the currycomb and John Marsh appeared, his hat still on his head this time and looking like a right cowboy.

"I didn't know you was there," he said.

"Papa was continuing to bend your ear, is why," I said.

John Marsh smiled at this but tried to make his face go straight again real quick.

I said, "You can find that true and amusing if you want. He's not here to take offense."

John Marsh angled his head at me, trying to figure what to say or do next. He wasn't used to sass in a girl, I guess. Wasn't used to girls at all, maybe. I should have just blowed in his nose and nickered at him.

"He does go on some," John Marsh said, speaking low.

I concentrated on my currying, though it was merely for show since I was combing out the same bit of flank I'd been working on for a while. Dixie looked over her shoulder at me, pretty much in contempt. I shot her a just-stand-there-and-mind-your-own-business glance and she huffed at me and turned away. I went back to combing and didn't look John Marsh in the eye for a little while, not wanting to frighten him off by being too forward but getting impatient pretty quick with the silence. The eligible males I'd known since I was old enough for them to be pertinent to me had all been either silly prattlers or totally tongue-tied. This John Marsh was seeming to be among the latter and I brushed and brushed at Dixie's chestnut hair trying to send some brain waves over to this outsized boy, trying to whisper him something to say to me. *Which horse is yours*? Or, *You go around teaching, do you?* Or, *Is there a Christmas Eve social at the schoolhouse tomorrow that I could escort you to?* But he just stood there.

Finally I looked over to him. He was staring hard at me and he ripped off his hat the second we made eye contact.

"I'll be out of your way shortly," I said.

"That's okay," he said. "Take your time. She deserves it." And with this he patted Dixie on the rump.

"You hear that, Dixie?" I said. "You've got a gentleman admirer." Dixie didn't bother to respond.

"Where's your horse put up?" I said.

"Oh, he likes the outdoors. Horses do. It ain't too fierce tonight for him."

"My Sam—he's the gray down there—it took a long time for him to adjust to a barn. But I like him cozy even if it's not his natural way."

"I'd set him out on a night like this," John Marsh said.

"He's better off," I said.

"I'm sure you love him," John Marsh said.

We both stopped talking and I wasn't sure what had just happened, though I felt that something had come up between us and been done with.

John Marsh nodded to me and moved away.

I stopped brushing Dixie and I just stood there for a moment and then I put down the currycomb and moved off from Dixie and found John Marsh unrolling his sleeping bag outside Sam's stall.

I moved past him to the door. "Night then," I said.

John Marsh nodded and I stepped out under the stars.

Then it was the morning before Christmas and I'd done my currying the night before and I'd had a dream of empty prairie and stars and I couldn't see any way to go no matter how I turned and so I slept on and on and woke late. As I dressed, there were sounds outside that didn't really register, their being common sounds, a horse, voices trying to speak over the wind, and then Papa came in and said, "Well, he's gone on."

Mama said, "The boy?"

"Yep," Papa said. "He wants to make time to Montana. He's got grit, the boy. The sky west looks bad."

I crossed the parlor, past the oak table and Papa, something furious going on in my chest.

"I was his age once," Papa said.

Then I took up my coat and I was out the door. It was first light.

Papa was correct. To the west, the sky was thickening up pretty bad. A sky like this in Kentucky might not say the same thing to a man. Even thinking this way, I knew there was more than bad weather to my stepping away from our house and looking to where John Marsh had gone, maybe only ten minutes before, and me churning around inside so fierce I could hardly hold still. Then I couldn't hold still. I told myself I needed to warn him.

I dashed into the barn and Sam was standing waiting and I gave him the bridle and bit and that was all. There was no time. I threw my skirt up and mounted Sam bareback and we pulled out of the stall and the barn and we were away.

There was a good horse trail through the rest of our land and on out toward the Black Hills that rippled at the horizon when you could see it. But there was only dark and cloud out there now, which John Marsh could recognize very well, and Sam felt my urgency, straight from my thighs. I hadn't ridden him bareback in several years and we both were het up now together like this, with John Marsh not far ahead, surely, and we galloped hard, taking the little dips easy and Sam's ears were pitched forward listening for this man up ahead, and mostly it was flat and winter bare all around and we concentrated on making time, me not thinking at all what it was I was doing. I was just with Sam and we were trying to catch up with some other possibility.

But John Marsh must have been riding fast too. He wasn't showing up. It was just the naked prairie fanning out ahead as far as the eye would carry, to the blur of a restless horizon. What was he running so fast for? Had I frightened him off somehow? Was it so bad to think he might put his arms around me?

I lay forward, pressing my chest against Sam, keeping low before the rush of the air, and I heard Sam's breathing, heavy and steady, galloping strong with me, him not feeling jealous at all that I was using him to chase this man. I closed my eyes. Sam was rocking me. I clung to him, and this was my Sam, who wasn't a gray man at all, not a man at all, he was something else altogether, he was of this wind and of this land, my Sam, he was of the stars that were up there above me even now, just hiding in the light of day, and we rode like this for a while, rocking together like the waves on the sea, and when I looked up again, there was still no rider in sight but instead an unraveling of the horizon. Sam knew at once what my body was saying. He read the faint tensing and pulling back of my thighs and he slowed and his ears came up and I didn't even have to say for him to stop.

We scuffled into stillness and stood quiet, and together Sam and I saw the storm. All across the horizon ahead were the vast billowing frays of a blizzard. I had a thought for John Marsh. He'd ridden smack into that. Or maybe not. Maybe he'd cut off for somewhere else. Then Sam waggled his head and snorted his unease about what we were looking at, and he was right, of course. He and I had our own life to live and so we turned around and galloped back.

The storm came in right behind us that day before Christmas in 1910, and there was no social at the schoolhouse that year. We all burrowed in and kept the fires going and sang some carols. *Stars were gleaming, shepherds dreaming. And the night was dark and chill.*

After midnight I arose and I took a lantern and a shovel and I made a way to the barn, the new snow biting at me all the while, but at last I came in to Sam and hung the lantern, and he muttered in that way he sometimes did, like he knew a thing before it would happen—he knew I'd be there—and I lay down by my horse and I put my arms around him. "Aren't you glad you're in your stable," I whispered to him. "I brought you here away from the storm." And I held him tight.

The Swing

by Margaret McMullan

Catch lit a joint and smoked it as he drove past the Gulf Coast Pak & Ship, which still had its sun-faded WE SHIP FOR THE HOLIDAYS sign up from last year. It was Friday, Christmas Eve, and he was going to fetch his holiday bonus from Mr. Zimmer in the big yellow house, his last paycheck for the week. Squinting from all the light coming off the Gulf, Catch smiled, and his fingers slid along the steering wheel, anticipating those crisp new bills Mr. Zimmer would count out from his silver money clip.

He passed the old-people's home, and through his open window he could smell the stuffing and sweet potatoes cooking. He always did like mushy food, and he laughed, thinking about what a good old person he would be. He snuffed out his joint, slipping the charred nub into a Ziploc bag for later, and reached into the passenger seat for some cheese crackers and beef jerky. He still had the open box of Satsuma oranges and divinity cookies from Mrs. Gimbel and the sugared pecans from Mrs. Anderson. He'd save those for later. A man on a bicycle wearing a Santa hat waved, and Catch waved back.

In the Zimmers' drive, Catch slammed his truck door shut, straightened his hat, and laughed out loud at the Christmas display on the lawn next door: Santa was riding in his sleigh, holding a whip to the reindeer, while two white wire angels with flashlights stood in front of the sleigh, looking like those people who guide planes in for landings.

Around back the Zimmers' grown daughter was swimming laps in the heated pool, steam dancing off the surface of the water. She slogged back and forth without once stopping or looking up. The daughter's young son sat in a wheelbarrow parked next to the pool, reading a science book bigger than his head.

"Hey, partner," Catch said.

"Hey," the boy said, his mouth going back into the little green scarf someone had wound around his neck. What was his name again? He was tiny and blond, and his eyes were big like his mother's, and his mother's mother's. He looked like he wanted to smile but couldn't; like he thought he had to ask permission.

"Excited about all the presents you're going to get?"

The boy nodded. There was silence, and then the boy asked, "How are you?"

Catch wasn't used to a seven-year old talking this way, and he had to get used to the boy again. Teddy—that was his name. This kid wasn't stupid and not a bit shy, but if the Zimmers weren't careful, he was going to turn into a wormy, womany sissy. Catch liked to give it to him straight. "How am I, you say? Could be better. Could be worse. I'm still standing. Still breathing. I call that a victory."

Teddy looked curiously at Catch, then tucked his mouth back into his scarf.

Catch inspected the green yard he'd seeded with rye grass a month earlier. He'd learned to anticipate what homeowners needed. There were a lot of house-proud people in this neighborhood. Catch could fit five trailers like his inside the Zimmers' house. He had heard that Zimmer was of German extraction, not Jewish like he thought. He didn't know where all the money that had landed on this street came from, but he figured either out-of-state sugar or oil. Nobody ever made that kind of money in Mississippi; you had to leave, make your money, then bring it back with you. Some of these folks lived on the Gulf year round, but there were others, like the Zimmers, who came down for the winter. They needed a local to keep up the house and the lawn. Catch often wondered why the Zimmers kept coming back here, why they didn't get a place in, say, California.

The little porch on the martin house was rotting off. The birdhouse was made to look like the big house, and Catch felt obligated to keep it looking as nice, but Mr. Zimmer wanted him to concentrate on the big jobs: trimming the boxwood around the tennis court and cutting back the line of bamboo. Last Christmas, Mrs. Zimmer had ordered a fancy swing from a catalog, but with so much on her mind, she'd left it outside on the ground for a month, and after all the rains, the seat cupped and split. Catch told Mrs. Zimmer he could make a better swing himself anyway.

Leave it to him; he'd get around to it. He'd even picked the perfect live oak to hang it in.

The Zimmers' kitchen door opened, and oniony smells wafted out; there was Mrs. Zimmer, looking frantic.

"Catch," she said. "Oh, I'm so glad you're here." She gave him an envelope. "That's for the month, and there's your bonus too. Now I know it's your day off, but I need you today and tonight. Could you help? Please? The lawn needs mowing again, and we can't put up the tree by ourselves. We've got guests coming over at six. And tomorrow's Christmas. I just don't know if I can manage. Do you want to come in for coffee? Have you had breakfast?"

Mrs. Zimmer wasn't quite like the other retired women. Lady up the street wouldn't even let Catch inside her house; at lunchtime she opened a can of Vienna sausages and dumped them out on a paper plate, then handed the plate to Catch with some saltines, like she was feeding a cat. Catch was a white yard man. He wondered what that woman had fed the black men who'd worked for her before him.

Catch tipped his hat, said he'd had breakfast, and sure, he could take the mower for a once around.

Riding the John Deere, he lit the rest of his joint: just enough to make the morning feel like a celebration. The air was cold and hurt Catch's teeth. At least it wasn't August or September, when he would have been sweating into his eyes. Riding a mower and smoking some weed the day before Christmas suited Catch just fine. Pot was the only drug he liked to mess with. His former boss at the lumberyard had had a bad cocaine habit. Catch could deal with just about anything but that. One morning his boss had knocked the cowboy hat off Catch's head and lit into him, yelling and waving a knife. Catch punched him in the face, good and solid, then picked up his hat and left. That was the end of that job.

After Catch finished mowing, he went back up to the house to see what else Mrs. Zimmer needed. She stepped outside, holding on to the screen door so it wouldn't slam. Catch thought she looked to be moving much better after the hip surgery. She had put on a few pounds, but the weight looked good on her. So did the tangerine lipstick and the blue flowered dress. Mrs. Zimmer didn't study Catch the way the other old women did, the way Catch was used to being studied. He knew what they thought of him. He lived alone; he drank. Some knew about the dope, but most didn't. Everyone knew he was quick to anger. He got into fights. He got kicked out of places. Some might have felt sorry for him. He knew he wasn't *happy* happy. He knew people studied his kind of not-happiness—he didn't want to call it *un*happiness or depression or post-traumatic stress disorder: he'd been like this before the two tours in Vietnam.

"I know this is your day off, Catch, but can you help with the tree too?"

"Help" meant put it up. Mrs. Zimmer liked to tell people Catch "helped" with the yard and the gardening when, in fact, he did it all. He never bothered correcting her of course.

The tree lay on the back porch, or what Mrs. Zimmer called "the gallery," and Catch knelt on the cold marble and screwed last year's stand onto it. Upright, the tree was small and bushy. He wondered how much the old lady had paid. She'd probably been ripped off.

"Oh, it's perfect," she said, as he hauled it in from the porch.

He would have gotten a bigger one, taller. Why else have twelve-foot ceilings like that?

"Can you put on the strings of lights too? We're only doing red and silver decorations this year."

Catch opened the lights and colored balls and put them all on the tree. At the last minute, the old woman gave him one more box to hang: twelve sea-glass ornaments, a gift from a woman named Nelia.

"Oh, that's perfect, Catch, perfect. I don't know how you do it." She handed him a package.

"Thank you, Mrs. Z. You oughtn't have," he said, thinking the bundle felt too light for a ham.

"I was wondering if you could put it on. For tonight. We're hoping you could play Santa at the party. It just wouldn't be Christmas without a Santa."

Catch opened the package. It was a lot of red inside.

"You'll be a Victorian Saint Nick," she said, staring down at the red velvet suit in his hands. "It wasn't a cheapy."

Outside, the daughter was still swimming laps in the pool. It made Catch's head hurt just watching her. Why did people make their lives more difficult than they already were?

Catch drove home to eat lunch and think. He lived in a trailer park but was saving up for a nice brick ranch house on the bay. He wanted his own dock and a motorboat, so he could go fishing first thing in the morning, maybe take the boat to Wolf River if he had a mind to.

He boiled three hot dogs and, still carrying the Santa package, took a seat on the lone aluminum chair out front. There was no grass, but he kept the ground swept. He didn't mind the passing trains so much anymore, not when he thought of how he would have the boat soon enough. Between his trailer and the train tracks he grew tomatoes and peppers in tires, coffee cans, and milk jugs cut in half. He popped open a beer and breathed in the smell of sweet olive, magnolia, and pine. He knew he drank too much, because lately he felt old in the mornings. One day he'd quit.

Part of the beard hung from the package, tickling his thigh. He opened the box. The beard was big and curly, but they'd skimped on the boots: vinyl flaps that strapped onto a regular shoe. There were some things that just shouldn't be.

Mrs. Zimmer was waiting for him on the front porch, and when she saw Catch in the suit but still wearing his work boots, she said no, no. She noticed things like shoes. He strapped on the flaps.

Mrs. Zimmer led Catch into the house through the front door. The living room was all lit up, and there were more people there than he'd expected: older people with no kids, neighbors from front and back and sideways. He mowed lawns for many of them, maybe one square mile all together. Shrimp and oysters on the half shell sat for the taking in a big crystal bowl full of ice. He didn't know why the Zimmers put out such a fine spread for people he was sure didn't appreciate it. Why didn't they just do like that old man down the street did? On Christmas Day, he gave any relative who came by a hundred dollars. Catch got fifty and a pie. No muss, no fuss.

"Pardon me," Teddy said. He had a gap in his smile where his two front teeth were out; the new teeth were coming in crooked. "Are you Santa Claus?"

"You bet, partner. How about you tell me what you want for Christmas."

"I think you're supposed to sit down first," the boy said. Mr. Zimmer came into the room with two drinks. "But not in that chair. Grandfather doesn't like for people to sit on that chair. It's from some other century, not this one."

Mr. Zimmer told Teddy to get Santa some gumbo, and he led Catch to a big leather wing-back chair and put a hot toddy in his hand. Then Mr. Zimmer counted out three twenties, a ten, and a five from the wad of money in his clip. No wallet, this guy. Catch tucked the cash into the pocket of his red velvet suit and sipped the toddy. He overheard a lot of talk about the hurricanes they'd had in Florida that year: Charley and Frances. "They had to gut Emma's condo because of the mold," one woman said to Mrs. Zimmer. Teddy came with a cup of gumbo. Catch took a taste. Someone in that kitchen knew how to burn a roux good. *Lord*

Almighty! he thought. Right now, he could drink up the afternoon.

One wall of the room was all glass, and Catch could see the whole Gulf of Mexico from where he sat. Even though the water was polluted, it was pretty to look at and think on. When he'd been married, he and Linda would spread out a blanket and picnic there on the beach, smoke a little weed, then lie back, close their eyes, and just listen. It was only a drab little spot of sand, but the sound of the water was just the same as it would have been on some Hawaiian island. Those were the best nights in Pass Christian—you all but forgot about the poisons in the water.

Mr. Zimmer plopped the kid on Catch's lap. Catch knew he smelled of weed, and what with the hot toddy and the gumbo on his bad stomach, he hoped to God he didn't get sick.

"It's Christmas Eve," the boy said. "Shouldn't you be working?"

"I am, son. And what do you want for Christmas?"

The boy shrugged. "I don't know."

Catch looked around the room, where everything and everyone sparkled. Someday it would all belong to this little kid. He wouldn't even have to ask for it. It was just automatic, a fact of life. It would be his. "I suppose you don't have to want anything," Catch said. "Used to be all I wanted for Christmas was snow."

"I sort of already know what I'm going to get. Santa always brings me lots of new books and clothes, a new coat, and maybe a ball. And Mom gives me candy and new stationery for thank-you notes. Last year it was Curious George." He sniffled, then reached into his pocket and pulled out some blue Kleenex covered in penguins.

"Well what more is it you want? Hell, kid, you got everything right here."

The boy looked at Catch with a you-don't-get-it-do-you? look. "There aren't any kids to play with."

"Maybe you're just a little homesick," Catch said as the boy blew his nose. "I heard a nasty rumor. I heard you *like* Chicago."

"I live there. You ever been?"

"Once, in 1992. Too many people. Too many people where I'm at now, too. I plan to move further up north."

"Norther than the North Pole?"

"Ah . . . yeah."

"You don't like people?"

"No real need for them. Look. Kid. Ted. Let's figure out what you want for Christmas, huh?"

"I don't know what's wrong with my mom. She acts mad all the time, ever since Dad left."

Catch looked across the room at the kid's mom, a good-looking woman, her skin saggy not from age, but from weight loss. She'd married and divorced some Chicago Yankee who used to show up on holidays with all those fruit-named gadgets, like apple and blackberry: little computers that turned into phones; phones that took pictures. Now he wasn't showing up anymore.

"All my life I've been trying to get away from this place," the daughter said to some neighbors, her eyes faintly circled with the red indentations from her swim goggles. Someone needed to feed that poor woman a plate full of red beans and rice with some good andouille sausage, or maybe just a steak. "She's just disappointed is all," Catch said to Teddy. "Haven't you ever been disappointed?"

The kid thought for a minute. "I went to a birthday party once, and they didn't have cake."

"That's what I'm talking about. Sucks, don't it?"

The kid showed Catch a clip attached to the buttonhole of his shirt. The clip looked like it might hold a mitten to a coat sleeve. "This is where I keep my lucky rock. I clip it here. Then it sucks out the luckiness, which gets into my coat, which is next to my sleeve, which is next to my arm skin, and I get charged with the luck, and then I am powerful."

"All right. Now you're thinking," Catch said. "Anything else on your mind?"

"Why do people swing their arms when they walk?"

"Jesus, kid, I don't know. Helps them keep moving, I guess."

"Making your list, checking it twice?" Mr. Zimmer said, putting another hot toddy in Catch's hand. God bless him.

"You have a lot of hair on your hands," the boy said. Catch's nails were dirty too. They were always dirty from work the day before, and the day before that.

"Yeah, well. So what do you want for Christmas?"

The boy shrugged. "A surprise is all."

"Come on, kid. Ask for something big. Your granddaddy—I mean, I can get my elves to make you anything. How about a BB gun?"

"I'm not allowed."

Catch could hear an old woman he used to work for giving somebody details he didn't want to hear about her woman surgery. She sighed loudly, shook her drink, and said, "Really, at my age, all you've got left is your posture and your jewels."

"All right then. How about a treehouse?"

"Grandmother says it will ruin her view."

Catch nodded and gulped his drink. Mrs. Zimmer hobbled toward them, smiling. There were lines on her soft, pale face where she'd been smiling all her life. "Santa, please have some more to eat, or another drink.

"No, Mrs. Z. I've got too much to do tonight. You and I both know I'm on duty." Catch winked and then lifted the boy from his lap. The boy whispered in Catch's ear, "I think my grandmother's hard of hearing."

"Well, that happens when folks get old," he whispered back to the boy. "We lose stuff along the way."

The wind off the Gulf was colder now, and as Catch drove back up the highway, still wearing the Santa suit, he wished he had saved the rest of that joint. He considered going to the casino—maybe he could double the money in his pocket. He pulled off onto a quiet street, stopped the car, and got out to vomit. He puked up all of it: gumbo, oysters, shrimp, everything. A dog came trotting by and started eating up the mess, which made him puke all over again. He got some on his suit, and he wondered briefly how he would clean it.

Catch stopped at a gas-station pay phone to call a girl he knew, but he got her machine. "Hey," he said into the phone after the beep. "It's just me. I was wondering if you was home or what." When he got back in the car, he regretted the call and headed for the McDonald's drive-through, the only place still open at dinnertime on Christmas Eve. Hoping to settle his stomach, he ordered up a big dinner, paid, and drove off without it. Halfway home, he realized he'd forgotten his food, and he went back.

"Pardon me," he said to the girl taking the orders. After he said it, he remembered these were the same words Teddy had used. The words sounded strange to Catch in his own voice. He explained to the girl what he'd done and tried to laugh at himself. As he waited at the window for her to put his order together again, he looked inside to see his ex-wife, Linda, standing at the counter. She was wearing a blue velour jogging suit and ordering, he was certain, a Filet-O-Fish sandwich. It was what she always ordered when she was high on something. No way did he want her to see him now, smelly and dressed as he was.

After he got his food, he parked across the public park facing the Gulf and started in on his fries. Used to be he and Linda would swing on those playground swings and walk that very beach. She left after she hooked up with her dealer. She was high and swearing a blue streak the day she left, throwing her things into a big plastic garbage bag, yelling until her voice finally got cut off by the door as she slammed it behind her.

A car passed on the street, and Catch could feel the thumping rap music in his loins. Some kids in the car threw Mardi Gras beads, which hit the hood of Catch's pickup. People around here, they got a little money, and they went out and bought cellphones, DVD players, and sound systems for their cars. As far as Catch could tell, it all ended up at the pawnshops near the casinos.

He unwrapped his first burger and bit into it. There was no meat, just bread, sauce, and lettuce. The other two were the same way. *Ha-ha to you too*, he thought, sure this was some damn joke that McDonald's girl had played on him. Maybe Linda had even had something to do with it. This stuff didn't just happen by accident. Nothing just happened.

Catch turned the key in the ignition. He had a mind to go back and ram the place with Linda in it. He hit his steering wheel hard, honking the horn. In the distance a horn honked back. Dogs barked, and someone yelled, "Merry Christmas!" He caught a glimpse of his fake white beard in the rearview mirror, the curls dirty and sagging around his neck. He took a deep breath and let it out with a cough, then turned off the engine, opened the windows, and looked again at the Gulf.

Back in Khe Sanh, his best friend had a Zippo lighter engraved with the motto: "If I had a farm in Vietnam and a home in hell, I'd sell my farm and go home." Catch had kept the lighter after he'd zipped up his friend in a body bag.

Catch thought about what the Mississippi Sound was made of. There it was, half the country's rivers spilling their guts out into the Gulf of Mexico, the ocean waters taking on the world's poisons, the whole of it creeping back with the tide, inching its way toward land like so many injured soldiers crawling home. Dying waters, but not dead yet, going back and forth, up and down the beach. And every now and again, a hurricane came along, and those sorry waves partied hard on the land, flattening beach houses, wiping the earth clean.

And slowly Catch started missing his ex-wife; not so much Linda, as just having a wife. A buddy of his had told him once about how French girls came in groups to the Mississippi Gulf Coast back in the 1700s, chaperoned by Ursuline nuns. They were called the *casquette* girls, because they came with suitcases to marry French settlers. Better than mail-order brides, these French girls were carefully selected, skilled, and pious, and some of the proudest Creole families trace their ancestry to them. They made a movie about it years ago, a musical in black and white. Looking out at the horizon, Catch felt like one of those early settlers now, and just as those brides had come to all those lonely men, he hoped some big idea would come to him and make his life better.

On Christmas morning, in the dark of predawn, Catch snuck into the Zimmers' backyard, a knife in one hand and his flashlight in the other. He'd gotten a good, solid board, weatherproofed and treated. He had good rope too, thick and sturdy, and he carried all this in the pack on his back. He would have worked faster without the dope, but still, in a little over an hour, he put the swing together right. Recalling how the boy's legs hit him midshin, he adjusted the height just so.

"Oh, Catch. Catch." Mrs. Zimmer stood on her back gallery with a tray of rolls and coffee. She poured him a cup and put it in his hands. "Merry Christmas. I'm so glad you stopped by."

They watched the boy swing higher and higher, the toes of his red footed pajamas almost touching the tree's leaves.

"Do you think that branch is secure?" Mrs. Zimmer said.

"Oh, it'll hold."

"Santa knew, didn't he?" Mrs. Zimmer said, smiling up at him.

Catch would always remember this moment. He thought so even then. And when he'd come back a year later to see the wreckage from Katrina, to see how the boardwalk from the Gulf had landed in the backyard, along with the bits and pieces of furniture and house, Catch would stand there in wonder to find that swing still hanging from that tree, unharmed.

Catch cupped his hands over his mouth and shouted to Teddy,

"What's it look like from up there?"

"You and grandmother look like ants," the boy shouted back.

"Suits us just fine."

Mrs. Zimmer touched his arm. "Do you think you could help me take out all these boxes? The presents I had shipped for everybody came so overpackaged."

"Now? Won't the kid see and start asking questions about, you know, Santa and all?"

"Oh, I hadn't thought about that. But surely he doesn't still believe. You think?"

They watched the boy slow the swing down, scraping the grass with his toe, then push off again.

"Tell you what. I'll get those after he goes back into the house."

"Catch, you're wonderful. I don't know how you do it."

"Mrs. Z., about the Santa suit. I need to get it cleaned before I return it."

Mrs. Zimmer shook her head. "Keep it, Catch. You're a natural. Save it for next year."

He laughed and said, "Now, just wait a minute, Mrs. Z."

But Mrs. Zimmer touched his arm, and Catch put his hand on top of hers. This was before Katrina took away the Zimmers and the town and all those other people he'd just gotten to liking. This was before. And for that moment, the two of them stood there on the back gallery, smelling the jasmine growing up alongside the house and watching the boy swing.

Luke

by Sheryl Cornett

Alan pulls his Silverado into Rachel's ridiculous driveway: semicircular, asphalt, unnecessary. Probably 10k worth, and on this still-dark morning it's icier than a skating rink—a lot icier than the main roads, which haven't even been salted after last night's freezing rain. At least it's clearing up now: full moon's still high and spreads its milky light like a mantle over the blacktop.

My God—he says to the cold dark morning—what am I doing with a woman who puts in an asphalt semicircular driveway out here in the middle of nowhere? Alan asks this question every time he's out here to pick her up. Rachel, an attorney and self-aware convert to Judaism. Hell, her religion mattered less than her being a lawyer, even his mother and sisters admitted that much just the other day. And since this in itself was a real step forward for anyone in his own family he took it as a sign. It *had* to be a sign, because he and all his relatives had always believed that the only attorney to be trusted (theirs) was one who did land deals and closings on farms they'd been buying up since the Depression. His mother accepting Rachel's religion *and* her profession was a changing of the guard. He didn't know what all to make of it. Wonders never cease—her Baptist ways had kept him from growing a beard for a good many years, and now here she was approving of his Jewish-lawyer girlfriend. Next she *would* be accepting this beard he'd grown, by God, at the age of fifty-two. Why shouldn't he have? She'd have to get over it because this was the new man and besides he planned to groom it over the next year and enter the Hemingway look-alike contest up at the hunt club. It isn't vanity, it's a fact, to admit he looks younger *and* more up-to-date with the facial hair—even women in the Bible loved all the guys with beards. It's a sexiness as old as time.

It's 5:14 a.m. by the light of the digital green clock on the dashboard. The stars still shine in the jet-black sky as he pulls into her out-of-place driveway so he can collect the boy and take him hunting. He sees Luke now, watching for him through the plate-glass bay window. The sight of the boy makes him nervous; he drinks a slug of the velvety coffee keeping him company in a stainless-steel mug on the dash.

Ten-year-old Luke stands in the curtainless shadows. He doesn't come out to the truck straight away, appears to be zipping and unzipping coat pockets. But you can tell he's been watching for Alan's headlights, and sure enough, the angle of the truck beams light through the bay window, into the den, so we see when Luke turns to head out the door.

He climbs into the cab, producing two sausage biscuits from his zip pockets. As he peels off their microwave wrap, they smell up the cab with pork fat growing cold. He hands one to Alan.

"Are you my mom's boyfriend?" Luke asks, biting into the half unwrapped sandwich, then setting it on the dash next to Alan's coffee—above the digital clock, which now says 5:18. He buckles his seatbelt, rubs his hands together like an old man in front of the woodstove. "Don't this heater work?"

Alan cranks it up a notch.

"Well, are you? Mom's boyfriend?"

Glad to keep his eyes on the road, Alan returns: "I don't know. Can't really say."

"Well, you're not the only one who wants to be."

"I know that. I am well aware of that." The steering wheel seems to expand in Alan's hand, whitening his knuckles.

"Are you taking me hunting because you want to get on my mom's good side?" Luke fingers the compound bow riding in the window rack above the truck seat.

"Maybe that is part of why I'm taking you out here today. But I also know you like hunting. You never know. Could be a little of both." There, he'd taken the upper hand.

Winn-Dixie up ahead on the left marks his turn. The red and white sign, reminding the world that Winn-Dixies are the beef people, is wreathed and roped in silver tinsel. It commands passersby to reserve their turkeys NOW, though today is New Year's Day, the holidays officially over and done with. This is good news to Alan, the holidays—their twinkly brightness—exhaust him, but he still hates to see them go. Their end signifies hunting season's nearly over, too.

"I like hunting," Luke says. The words hang like the ice bending tree branches as far as the eye can see. "I appreciate it. Going hunting. But I don't need a step-daddy."

"Keep your eyes peeled for a gravel road just up here to your right—it's easy to miss," Alan directs. There it is—he'd forgotten the new BP station, too much garish green and yellow up against the thick woods along the two-lane highway. He'd been in there once and felt he was in a mini Wal-Mart—they sell everything in that BP: car batteries, Christmas decorations (year-round), home pregnancy tests. Seized suddenly by the desire to go in and check out what new stock they carried, Alan found himself sweating in restraint. Right now at 5:33 a.m. on January 1, he's got this urge to go into that mini Wal-Mart and keep on itemizing the inventory.

"Is that your road there?" Luke asks pointing. He unzips another coat pocket and takes out two more biscuits, undoing their plastic wrap, which has gone cold and comes off easily now.

Again, Luke offers one of the biscuits to Alan.

"Thank you."

"You're welcome."

Lord! He's a polite boy, handsome, too—dark smooth skin, those big eyes with which he keeps staring at Alan. He'd sometimes wondered if he himself had some fruit of a union out there and just didn't know it. Maybe back from before he was married and divorced. That's a thought he liked to think sometimes. Maybe he had a son out there somewhere, one who would come and find him in his old age.

With his teeth, Alan tries to unwrap the remaining plastic off his biscuit. Luke reaches over, untangles the bundle, and passes it back for Alan to finish off.

"Thank you," Alan is glad to say something other than responding to the step-daddy statement. Luke's expectation of a response stands out there between them like yet another biscuit. Alan feels the child's eyes on him—probably checking out the beard, comparing him to the lawyer geeks his mother usually goes out with. Alan also knows through Rachel that Luke, as a rule, has nothing to do with men she dates. So this hunting gig is something, and Alan remains as surprised at the opportunity as he is that Rachel says she enjoys his company, claims to want a hands-on kind of guy, someone down to earth. She didn't hold against him that he'd never put to use his marketing degree.

Luke's eyes remain on him; Alan's keep landing on the dashboard clock—it's now 5:42—as onto a touchstone for confidence. What was the boy looking at? Did he see someone too old for his mother? A man from a different world, a carpenter's world of sawdust and power tools and fall weekends seeking eight-point-rack trophies? Rachel never stopped asking about hunting—she wanted to go with him some day soon—but Alan had to wonder sometimes if she was just fascinated by and experimenting with him.

The eastern horizon is gaining some gray. 5:46 a.m. The moon lowers herself to bed.

"I'm not only Jewish and Christian," Luke offers, sucking boxed juice through a straw, his mouth full of biscuit. "I'd like to be an atheist, too. But then I'd have to give up Christmas and Chanukah. At least that's what Mama Gwen says. She don't like my mom taking me to temple, either. Still Mama Gwen always brings up Christmas and Chanukah when she's lecturing me. You can't be an atheist and still have Christmas or Chanukah, either one; and if you stop believing, you stop receiving. That's what she says every year. So I figure, better safe than sorry. I rededicate my life at least once a year at Mama Gwen's VBS—she's in charge of the whole thing, every year. My mom says not a word about it either, not one word. So between temple and VBS I keep them both happy."

Alan pulls the truck off the gravel road onto a flat clearing, leaving the engine running for the heater. The cab is so warm now he's sweating at the temples and the back of his neck.

"Well, sounds like you've got your bases covered." Should they get out of the truck now? Is the boy through talking? The light is perfect—dusty rose magnified by the iced branches—there'll be full sun before long, but for the next hour the deer'll be looking for whatever vegetation they can find that's not sheathed in ice. It tugs on him, the light does; he wants to get out there, climb up into the tree stand, stare into the woods. Alan continues, "Yep, you sure do have your bases covered."

"Sure I do. That's what I'm thinking, too."

"You know, Luke, Jesus had a step-daddy."

Silence, then, till the truck's engine fan kicks in.

"I know that," Luke says. "Joseph is Jewish and he's a big part of the Christmas thing. I was the baby Jesus once when I was five months old. Mama Gwen signed me up for the pageant before I was born. So I know it: Mary and Joseph—you take them out of the mix and you got no story. They're real important. Joseph just as much as Mary. It goes both ways."

"So there you go: Step-daddies can't be that bad if Jesus had one."

During the pause that follows, Alan looks toward the lake and the ice-covered tree trunks, iridescent like pillars made from mother of pearl.

Luke shadows Alan's gaze for a bit, then says: "No. Guess not. Hadn't thought of it that way before." He zips the pockets and hood of his parka. "Is your tree stand a two-seater?"

"Sure is." The clock clicks to 5:55. "Let's go get us a buck."

"I'm ready."

The man and the boy get out of the truck. They walk east through the trees, toward the now alabaster light reflecting off the lake, where soon the sun will rise.

The Amaryllis

by Mary Ward Brown

It came to be the first thing he thought of each morning. What did it do overnight?

He would get up and go straight to the parlor for a quick look. More fascinated each day, he would hurry through breakfast, then take his second cup of coffee back to sit and study the newest development.

The amaryllis was now two feet tall, its first lilylike bloom the diameter of a salad plate and a twin bloom rapidly opening to the same glowing red. There was also a slightly lower second stalk with three heavy buds still to come.

The whole thing was so beautiful it had come to dominate the entire house. It was not only alive but dramatically alive. It had presence, almost like a person, and he was conscious of it off and on all day. More and more, however, it seemed to be asking something of him, he wasn't sure what.

Today, Thursday, with the bloom at its peak and the bud half open, he got the message. He couldn't have something that special in the house and not share it. But with whom? The question had flawed every good thing that happened since Margaret died.

Margaret would have loved the amaryllis, but all the other appreciators he could think of were either busy working, far away, or dead.

Their son Angus, was as worthy as Margaret, in his way, but he was both busy and far away. Still, the thought of Angus with the flower was irresistible. At seven-fifteen he dialed the house. Mary Ann answered.

"Oh, Judge Manderville?" She was surprised, also anxious.

"Nothing is wrong," he assured her. He never called in the morning except in an emergency. "I wanted to invite you all down for the weekend. I have something to show you."

"*This* weekend?" Silence. "Angus has already gone, Judge Manderville. He has surgery this morning. But I know we can't come. We're all involved, the children too. What do you have to show?"

"Remember the amaryllis bulb you gave me? It's blooming and it's unbelievable."

She laughed. "I know. It's a hybrid from California. Did I tell you?"

"Yes. But you didn't prepare me for anything like this. Maybe I couldn't have been prepared. It's the most beautiful thing I ever saw."

"I'm glad you like it, Judge Manderville. Angus will be too. I'm really sorry we can't come. It'll be a while, two or three weeks, before we can get away, I expect. You know how things are here."

He knew. He could see Mary Ann dressed for a nonstop day,

about to chauffeur his grandchildren to school, her time all planned straight through to dinner.

"Well, thanks, Mary Ann." He knew she had to go. "Sorry you can't make it. Love to everyone. Good-bye."

Going back for his coffee, now cold, he entered the parlor with a sense of apology, and left at once without looking at the flower. He hadn't really expected that they could come, so why was he disappointed?

His son had become almost inaccessible, he thought, as he washed up the dishes. He knew Angus was there but he no longer saw him except on holidays, parts of vacations, and when he was pressured into going for annual physicals. Angus belonged to his patients first and his immediate family second. The Judge no longer thought of himself as immediate.

Which was not really fair. Angus didn't like the distance between them. Sometimes he called as late as ten, apologized, and talked on. One night the Judge was awakened at ten-thirty to hear Angus saying, "I just called to say I miss you, Dad. Go on back to sleep." Angus' voice had sounded bone-tired and lonely, and the old father-sonship had flamed up to bring the Judge instantly awake and available. They had talked for an hour.

There was no doubt that Angus loved him. To Mary Ann he thought he must be something of an obligation, regularly and necessarily on the list but never quite convenient, certainly never a first choice. He felt she was fond of him and would visit him with reasonable regularity in the nursing home. She would see that he had a nurse, but she herself would not sit and hold his hand if the last days drew out.

His two grandchildren were beloved, close strangers. And the fact remained. He was quite alone in the world.

Hanging up the dish towel, he went to finish dressing. He could invite McGowin over to see the amaryllis. McGowin would look and never really see it. Then he would stay all day and talk about the past. "Listen, James, do you remember . . ." he would say, and launch into some long-ago episode. The Judge hadn't mentioned the amaryllis to McGowin.

In his study he tried to get down to work, as he liked to call the self-appointed task of going through the letters, papers, scrapbooks, diaries, and financial records collected in the house since the time of his parents.

"What do you do with yourself these days, Judge Manderville?" people asked him in the grocery store or on the street.

"Right now I'm cleaning out the attic," he would say, and smile.

After all those years on the bench, years of power and some prestige as circuit judge, it embarrassed him a little to say what he was busy with now, going through his and Margaret's letters and papers, trying to separate the wheat from the chaff.

On the desk before him now were several small memorandum books to be filed away or discarded. Margaret had been a reader who looked up words she didn't know, then wrote word and meaning in a small notebook. It was a habit like brushing her hair, to which he had paid no real attention.

Opening the first notebook, he saw she'd written *deciduous, synecdoche*, and *ankh*, with meanings. Then she wrote, *ubi sunt*, but gave no meaning. Why not? he wondered. What did it mean? Out of context, he had no idea.

Near at hand, the phone rang. In the large, empty house the telephone was his link with the outside world, with the living. He always picked up expectantly on the first or second ring.

"Good morning, James," said McGowin.

"Hello, Mack."

"What you doing?"

"Working. How about you?"

"Not working." McGowin chuckled. "It's my birthday."

"How about that! How many?"

"You don't know? I'm eight months ahead of you. Don't you remember I got to go to school a year before you did? But you skipped the fourth grade and caught up in the fifth."

"Congratulations, Mack. Happy birthday. Are your children coming down or anything?"

"No. But they called, and I got presents from everybody. Shirts, ties, pajamas. You know."

The Judge hesitated briefly. "What're you doing this afternoon?"

"Nothing. Why?"

"What about my coming over around four?"

"Fine! Sure, James. That'll be great. I'll brew us some Sanka."

"How do you feel on your birthday?"

"I feel like hell. I know I'm on the shelf for good and I can't get used to it. Can you?"

"No, I can't either."

"We retired too soon. We should have hung on longer. But I had that little stroke. And you wanted to take care of Margaret."

"Yes. I don't regret it."

"Well. Like Satchel Paige said, 'Don't never look back. Something might be gainin' on you.'" They both laughed. "I'll let you get back to work, James. See you later."

"Have a good day, Mack."

Feeling selfish and justified at the same time, he put the receiver back on the hook. If he'd asked McGowin over, it would have started something that would go on for the life of the amaryllis. For McGowin it would be merely an excuse for companionship.

Protecting himself, however, did nothing for the plant. Sitting up there in absolute silence, it projected pressure through the walls.

He stared out the study window, trying again to come up with appreciators. All still busy, far away, dead. He sighed and gave up.

For McGowin's birthday, he decided to call the bakery and get a cake to take over. A cake with candles to go with their decaffeinated coffee.

He didn't look at the amaryllis again until after supper, when he went up and turned on all the lights in the front of the house. He turned on crystal chandeliers, table lamps, all. In his mind's eye he could see the house as it looked from the street, an 1850 colonial cottage in its original setting of trees and boxwoods, all lit up as though guests were expected.

He took a seat on the sofa, in front of which the plant stood on a low table from which he and Margaret used to serve demitasses or port after dinner. They had never cared much for society, but entertained when they had to and enjoyed having friends for dinner until her heart problems stopped even that.

In the handsome room, in artificial light, the amaryllis seemed to have taken on glamour, like a beautiful girl all dressed up for the evening. All dressed up and no place to go, he thought.

The strange thing was, he'd never "felt" anything for a plant before. On the contrary, he'd dismissed them all as more or less inanimate like potatoes and turnips, not animate in the way of cats and birds. He had bought dozens of hospital chrysanthemums, often delivering them himself in their foil wrapping and big bows, but they had seemed more artificial than real.

The amaryllis was different, entirely. He liked just being with it. Because of its size, he supposed, it seemed to have individuality, and then he had watched it grow daily, with his naked eye. Looking at the blooms, he thought of words like *pure* and *noble*, and old lines of poetry like "Euclid alone has looked on *Beauty* bare."

In return, the plant seemed neither friendly nor unfriendly.

It was simply there in all its glory, however fleeting. It was the fleetingness, he thought, that put on the pressure.

He took off his glasses, dropped them in his shirt pocket, and rubbed a hand across both eyes. Then he turned off the lights, one by one.

Next morning the second bloom was wide open, as breathtaking as the first. Red was not his favorite color, but this red was both muted and vibrant, the color of a winter sunrise, or a robin's breast. The two blooms exuded a kind of concentrated freshness like early morning in the woods, a baby's skin, or eyes just waking from sleep. Pure, unblemished by anything yet to come.

He dressed before breakfast and, while drinking coffee, wrote a note to the postman. "Eddie: Can you spare a minute to look at something in the house? Just ring the bell. Thank you. J.M." He was making a list of names when Pot arrived.

Pot came on Fridays. Years ago he had come every day of the week, including Sunday, and Margaret had taught him to clean, cook, and serve to a fine point. She had wanted him called Potiphar, a fitting name she thought, but it seemed affected no matter who said it, so they soon settled for his nickname. Pot didn't need to work now. His children were successful and had bought him a house. He drew his pennies. But he still came one day a week out of their mutual dependence, the Judge supposed.

He and Pot had been through all kinds of ups and downs

together, on both sides, including the loss of their wives. They had even gone through civil rights together, with him on the bench and Pot's people in the streets. There was a time when Pot had said, "I got to stay out awhile, Judge. But you understand it ain't between me and you."

Today he met Pot at the back door. "Hurry up, I've got something to show you!"

"Morning, Judge. What you got?" Tall and lean to the bone, Pot looked the part of a king's officer, superannuated perhaps. He stood up to his years with a blend of dignity and submission. Age was becoming to him.

"Let's go to the parlor," the Judge said. At the door, he stepped aside for Pot to go first.

"It done bloomed," Pot said, smiling. "I never saw nothing like that before."

"Neither did I."

"Makes you feel like you ought to go down on your knees, don't it, Judge?"

"It does."

Pot sighed. "Well, I got to get on to the house." Bowing unconsciously, like an Anglican to the cross, he backed out of the room.

"I'm inviting some people in to see the flower," the Judge said as they went to the back hall. "Not many, maybe a dozen."

"You want to serve something?" Pot opened the closet door and got out the vacuum cleaner. He put on an attachment as carefully and precisely as if it were a saxophone.

"Coffee, maybe, if anyone wants it. But Mr. McGowin will be here for lunch, I expect."

"I'll take care of it."

A surge of love for Pot rose up in the Judge's chest, remained like a cramp as he put Eddie's note in the mailbox. How could he have overlooked Pot as an appreciator? Pot had looked at the flower with what it deserved, reverence.

He squared his shoulders and hurried to the phone with his list. If the elect couldn't come, he would get them from the highways and hedges. He put on his glasses and began to dial numbers, beginning with his nearest neighbor whom he never saw, separated as they were by three wooded acres.

He said approximately the same thing to each. "This is James Manderville. I have something here that you might like to see. It's a hybrid amaryllis in bloom, really beautiful. I hope you'll drop in if you can." Any time would be convenient, he said. He'd be at home all day.

And then he called McGowin. When it got down to bedrock, McGowin was all he had. McGowin said he'd be right over.

The rest of the day was a happening. McGowin arrived first, in a tweed coat and tie, his face red from chronically elevated pressure for which he took pills when he didn't forget them. He chose to sit on a chair opposite the amaryllis and stayed there all morning, a kind of noncirculating co-host.

When a lady entered the room, McGowin rose at once, a cross between southern gentleman and perpetual fraternity boy drilled in manners, and stood stalwartly until she sat down or left. He was fluent with anecdotes, flattery, and occasional wit, an old party man back in action.

The Buick dealer and his wife, neighbors, came around ten, the Buick dealer being his own boss, and able to take off at his pleasure. It was obvious that they were glad to be there, and to say later they had been. They did not come to see the amaryllis.

"I've seen them before, Judge," he said of the plant. "They come in other colors, too. Pink. White. Some are even variegated, but yours is beautiful.

"How old is this house, Judge? Did you inherit the antiques or collect them yourself? They're worth a fortune now. Look at those mirrors!"

His wife asked, "What kind of table is that, Judge Manderville, with the mirror below?"

It was called a "petticoat table," he explained, and why. He answered all questions and showed them the whole house. Then Pot served coffee. Their faces glowed with deference and interest. They had been here before, they told him as they left, but had never had a personal tour and they loved it. As they said, they had already seen an amaryllis.

As she started down the steps, the Buick dealer's wife looked him tentatively in the eye. "If you ever need anything, here all alone, you call us, Judge Manderville," she said. "Day or night."

"I may have to do that," he said. "And I won't forget. Thank you."

"I see your light at night through the trees, and I think of you often," she said. "Your wife was lovely."

Suddenly, to his great surprise, his eyes filled with tears and so, he saw, did hers.

The flower-shop owner, in the midst of making floral arrangements for a funeral, had to squeeze in her visit just before lunch. She wore a knit pantsuit, another squeeze, the Judge thought; she might as well have been stark naked. He caught a glimpse of McGowin's eyes. Poor old devil. He'd been a real ladies' man in his day and still got occasional calls from widows. But he no longer rose to the bait. After his wife died and the little divorcée turned him down, he seemed satisfied with, even somehow proud of, his bachelorhood.

The flower-shop owner was all business, however. "Do you know how much the bulbs cost, Judge? I'd like to get a few for the shop if they're not too expensive."

He said he'd get the address from Mary Ann and she could write the nursery. She sat long enough to drink a quick cup of coffee and smoke a cigarette.

"People pick the worst times to die," she said. "They wait until I have a wedding or a big party, like now. Then they all try to go at once.

And you know the old superstition, that if there's one there's got to be three? It never fails. I've seen it happen so often it scares me."

"Well, don't look at James and me," said McGowin. "We've got other plans."

At noon Pot called them in for T-bone steaks, baked potatoes, and a fine tossed salad. The Judge and Pot always ate well on Fridays, but the Judge usually did the cooking while Pot worked on the house.

"This is better than my birthday, James," McGowin said, looking around the table set with Spode and good silver.

They ate hungrily, saying little. McGowin cut his steak cleanly to the bone on both sides, eating fat and all, plus large chunks of French bread and butter.

"Bring out the rest of that cake, Pot," McGowin directed when they'd finished. "And light up the candles!"

"You brought your cake over, Mack?"

"Sure I did. I'm still celebrating, or holding my own wake, I don't know which."

With one quarter missing but with the candles lit, their small flames bowing over backward as he walked, Pot brought in the cake on a round silver tray. Ceremoniously he set it in front of McGowin and placed a cake knife beside it.

Catching the spirit, the Judge said, "Get out a bottle of cream sherry, Pot. Put it in a decanter."

Pot was smiling. Wearing the white coat he kept in the pantry for special occasions, he soon came back with a decanter of wine and two Waterford sherry glasses on a tray.

"Hot damn!" said McGowin. "Long live the big petunia—or whatever the hell its name is."

Since he drew laughter, McGowin was inspired to go on. "What do you think that thing is, Pot, male or female? It looks like a stud petunia to me, but it could be a liberated female. They outdo us every which way now, you know."

Eddie the postman rang the doorbell as if on cue. Pot went to let him in while the Judge and McGowin took their second glass of wine to the parlor.

Eddie was a fine appreciator. Standing straight as for the national anthem, he made a ringing statement. "That is the most beautiful thing I ever saw in my life, Judge Manderville. That is really something. I wish my wife could see it."

"Bring her over, Eddie," said the Judge. "Bring her, by all means."

"Just call before you come, Eddie," said McGowin. "So James will have his shoes on."

"His shoes, Mr. McGowin? Ha Ha. You're still a card!" Eddie came a few steps nearer McGowin, leaned down and said in a whisper intended for the Judge to hear, "I've known the Judge for years, you know. He's a real gentleman. A gentleman if I ever knew one."

"Scholar, too, Eddie." McGowin winked. "Don't forget that."

"Oh, yes, sir. A scholar, too. You should see the books and papers I bring him."

Eddie said he had no time for coffee or wine, though a glass of wine would certainly be nice. People had to have their mail on time or they got upset. All down the street they were waiting for him right now, he told them.

There were no more visitors until late afternoon. McGowin's body, struggling with too much food and alcohol, both forbidden, dragged down his spirit like a stone. He first began to nod, then put his head back on the chair and slept soundly, snoring from time to time. The Judge went back to his notebooks in the study. He too felt drowsy, but down the hall he heard the vacuum cleaner going. If Pot could work, so could he.

Ubi sunt was not in the dictionary they usually used. So that was it. Margaret had been reading in bed, probably, and hadn't felt like getting up for a word. In the unabridged dictionary, which badly needed dusting, he found it at once: "adj. (L. 'where are (they)?') Relating to a type of verse which has as principal theme the transitory nature of life and beauty."

Suddenly Margaret's workbooks became intimate, as if they were journals, in a way. Someone else would have to throw them out, he decided, not he.

He took out his handkerchief and dusted off the dictionary, then shook the handkerchief and put it back in his pocket. At his desk he pushed the wordbooks aside and sat staring out at the winter afternoon. The light of the desk lamp seemed to focus on his hands, quietly folded.

Soon after the hall clock struck four, McGowin appeared in the doorway, rumpled and dazed. "Any coffee left, James?"

"Yes. Let's have some."

They went to the kitchen, where a percolator of fresh coffee was set on "warm." At the kitchen table they drank a cup together, black, and in silence.

"Thanks, pal," said McGowin, draining his cup. "I got to be going."

"You'll miss the others."

"Can't help it, James. I'm through for the day. Has Pot gone?"

"No, but he should have finished by now. Would you give him a ride?"

"That's what I had in mind. Round him up."

McGowin drove a twelve-year-old Mercedes, but he drove it less and less, having been warned by the police about driving across yellow lines, turning into wrong lanes and onto one-way streets.

As he and Pot drove off, their faces said the party was over and they were tired. Their faces also said they'd been to many parties, that they were always over, and everyone went home.

The legal contingent arrived together after five, though not in full force. To be strictly ethical the Judge had kept his distance from other lawyers while in office. When he retired he might as well have died, he sometimes thought. Now only the district attorney and two young lawyers, with their wives, showed up. There was also the small daughter of one of the couples.

When the Judge asked the child's age, she grinned and held up four tender fingers.

The lawyers wanted drinks, not coffee, and the Judge was glad to have good Christmas scotch and expensive birthday bourbon to bring out. A happy hour was soon under way.

Both lawyers and their wives, however, took the amaryllis in stride. Sitting around it in the parlor, one wife quickly abstracted an article she had read.

"There's a whole new thing about plants now," she told them. "They're supposed to thrive on tender loving care. They like to have music played in the room, like to be talked to. It seems to be a proven thing. They want love and affection like everybody else. You should talk to it, Judge Manderville."

A lawyer, not her husband, interrupted. "But I also read where that talking-to business is explained. People breathe out carbon dioxide and plants breathe it in. So it's not a matter of TLC, but chemistry."

The amaryllis was dismissed. "Have you kept up with the house-trailer controversy, Judge?"

Opinions flew at him from the lawyers while their wives sat drinking, smoking, listening. The little girl sat on the floor beside her mother's chair, holding on to what appeared to be a French shopping bag filled with toys. She didn't take out the toys, however, but stared at the amaryllis. From time to time she changed her attention to a person or object in the room, but always brought it back to the flower.

The Judge noticed. After a while, he got up and moved to a chair beside the child.

"What do you think of my flower?" he whispered.

"I love it," she whispered back through a wide, tongue-cluttered smile, then ducked her head, blonde hair falling around her cheeks. From her hidden mouth she said something he couldn't hear.

"What, dear?" he asked.

Conversation had stopped and everyone was looking at the child.

She raised her head only enough to meet his eyes with her own. "I want to touch it," she said.

"Well, I think *it* would like that too." He led her to the flower and lifted her up.

"Easy now," cautioned the mother.

With one finger she reached out, gingerly touched a red petal as though it were hot, and laughed delightedly.

When the Judge put her down she didn't move. "I want to kiss it!" she cried.

Everyone laughed except the mother, who said, "We're going too far now."

But the Judge lifted her up again. "Kiss it easy, then," he said.

Wrinkling her nose to avoid the long, yellow-padded stamens, she pressed one cheek lightly against a bloom. Her lips missed altogether.

Her mother stepped up to lead her away.

"No!" The child stood stubbornly, close to tears. "I *want* it. I want to take it to my home!"

"Oh, Lord, here we go." The mother gripped the child's arm with authority. "Time to leave, Judge Manderville. It's been delightful. Come to see us soon. Promise me you will!"

On the porch, as his visitors walked away, the Judge heard the phone ring. It was Angus saying Mary Ann had told him he'd called, that they would try to come in two weeks and spend one night. The Judge could tell Angus was pleased to hear about his flower show, about guests having been in the house.

He made a quick check to see that all the doors were locked, then gathered up empty cups and glasses, over-flowing ashtrays. He took them all to the kitchen but left them unwashed, unemptied. Like McGowin and Pot, he was tired. Too tired even to eat, he decided.

As he undressed, however, he thought of the amaryllis alone in the parlor. In bedroom slippers, he went back and turned on a light. The flower stood as beautiful as ever. Carefully, he picked up the pot and carried it back to his bedroom, where he set it on a table in front of a window. From there he could see it first thing in the morning.

He slept soundly all night but woke up vaguely depressed. In front of the window, backed by candid morning light, the amaryllis's blooms were like heavy translucent bells. Their hue, lightest at the edges, grew deeper and darker in each secret throat. In the sunlight, the living veins were apparent as never before.

But were the blooms quite as fresh, really as perfect, as yesterday?

On the second stalk, all three buds were opening at once. Their promise, however, was not as exciting as the first. The composition of the whole plant—pot, blooms, stalks—was no longer as good, for one thing. The center of interest was being lowered and to the wrong place. He couldn't analyze the difference. He only knew that any change, or beginning of change, was already for the worse.

Each day the amaryllis continued to do something new but in a downhill direction. The first blooms passed their prime and began to age in the same way that people did, the Judge thought. There was the same pitiful withering around the edges, subtle drooping and shriveling, gradual letting go of form. The shrunken petals finally turned the color of purple veins in old legs and hung down like deflated parachutes.

The lower set of blooms was smaller than the first and seemed replicas, not originals. Petty princes, not majesty.

The Judge was vaguely ashamed that he lost interest in the plant toward the last. When all the blooms had died, he was told to stop watering the bulb and put it away in a dark place, or even outside in the ground.

When he cleaned and straightened the house for his children's visit, he put the pot in the back-porch pantry. Tall green leaves had grown up around the stalks, and they flopped over awkwardly, hanging off the pantry shelf by the side of empty fruit jars, obsolete ice-cube trays, discarded dishes, and cooking vessels with missing tops.

He was told to leave the pot in the pantry and forget it until next year, when he could bring it out, start watering, and the amaryllis would grow and bloom again. It seemed incredible, but all the gardeners and flower people assured him it was true.

The Christmas Monkey

by Glen Allison

She fingers the tiny ebony charm on her necklace as she gazes out the window at the Mississippi countryside rushing past us. I always wonder what she might be thinking when she does that. Then again, the mysteries of her mind have often thwarted my pondering during her nineteen years on the planet.

As we drive southward the length of my tortured state, my mind replays this annual journey. From the predawn launch of my truck out of my driveway a few blocks from Elvis's birthplace, we tunnel through the evergreens of the Trace, skirt the capitol with its holiday lights still aglow in the office buildings, then sling down Highway 49 until the pines grow scrubbier and the air grows saltier long before it's possible to inhale it from the Gulf waves.

"How many more years will we do this, Dad?" she asks. It's the first time she has asked this. Maybe her college psych courses have made her bold and brilliant.

Even though the truck's slack, worn windows make the wind whistle around our heads, I scoop her words into my ears but give her no reply. The answer is: Until you refuse to go. But I won't say that now. I'll wait until we cross the tracks and traverse the decades back to the scarred pain of those unprotected days.

We let the faithful truck carry us along until the exit looms in the harsh brightness of our southern winter. The curving departure from the highway gives me an excuse to glance at my daughter while checking the rearview mirror, enough to see she has relinquished her chin-jutting glare in my direction. Her face is slightly turned away from me now. I study the plane of her face before it curves out of sight around her cheekbone beneath her lashes. I feel that familiar pang of undeserved blessing of having brought this beautiful creature into the world.

Still caressing the carved monkey on her necklace, she turns to watch me again but, college smarts or not, she is too slow to catch my focus on her.

The pavement narrows as it draws closer to the water, but we don't go that far. We twist our way through smaller streets until we are riding next to the railroad tracks that parallel the beach, which lies a mile or so southward. Before long, we are there.

Everything looks different since the two storms have done their terrible dance across the landscape. But just as the passage of decades have failed to erase my homing beacon to this place, neither has the feminine wrath of those hurricanes altered the terrain so much that I could not find it, no matter how much I might have wished otherwise.

We always wait until the day after Christmas to come here. I would have made the drive on Christmas day, if not for her. But I have always opened the gifts with her, a tradition I never had growing up, just the two of us ripping paper and giggling around the tree these nineteen years.

I know enough about my brother and sister and their families to know that they have kept the same hollow gift-giving practice for the sake of their kids. We always get together, all three of our families, at Thanksgiving. It seems more appropriate for us somehow.

Finally, I spy the railroad bridge. I pull off the road next to the tracks. All of the underbrush and some of the trees here were scraped away by the storms. But this is the spot. It burned a melancholy memory on my soul long ago.

I am conscious of her watching me closely as I turn and look at the house. It has been repainted since Katrina passed over. The trees at the corners of the house stand taller now as they droop over the roof like sullen sentries. There is no mistaking that house. There has been no mistaking it for nearly two decades.

"Do you miss her?" she asks me. "After all this time?"

I look at her blankly. Is she asking about the mother she never knew?

"How long did your mother keep you here?" Ah, the grandmother she never knew. She has never asked this before. Her focus has shifted from me to the house on the other side of the tracks.

"Not long," I say. "Not long enough."

She says nothing else for a few moments, long enough for me to slip back in time. It matters not that the foliage is gone from the spot where we hid that day.

The kudzu wove a perfect hiding place. From across the street, the people searching our house could not see us: a trio of children hidden behind the tapestry of vines and leaves.

But the three of us could see them perfectly.

"Shhhh—the game's about over," I whispered to Shelly and Buzz.

My brother, Buzz, eight going on thirty, was watching the social workers go through the front door of the house. We could hear them all the way across the tracks and the road as they called out our names. Buzz smirked. "If they mess up my baseball cards, I'm punching holes in somebody's tires."

Little Shelly was peering not at the house but up at the power lines above the kudzu. "Y'all hush," she said with all her five-year-old authority. "I can't hear the monkey."

I glanced away from the house. My little sister was overbundled in two sweaters and a too-big coat to provide more than enough warmth for a Mississippi winter day. She clutched a hairless doll under her left arm and was slowly waving her right arm up at the branches and leaves above us, sighting along her arm like a rifle. She was whispering something now.

"What are you saying?" I asked her, my eyes focused across the street again.

Her sing-song canting went silent. "Nuffin."

I looked down at her, then knelt beside her in the dirt floor under the canopy of vines next to the railroad tracks. "Shelly," I said, "there is no monkey."

In the distance, the train moaned.

Shelly continued pointing her arm at the tangled branches above us. She was humming now.

I put my hand on her face and made eye contact with her. "Shelly, there is no monkey. Were you singing that song that Buzz made up?" I glanced at my brother, who was studying our house across the street. "Buzz, stop telling her the monkey will bring her Christmas presents."

My brother, still turned toward the house, pulled the cracked leather letter jacket tighter around his shoulders. "It's just one more day, Ben."

"You just lied to her, Buzz."

He swiveled his head toward me. The smirk was gone. "Just because you are twelve don't mean you can boss me!"

It was a bit of lore in our neighborhood that a monkey had escaped from a pet shop and lived in the trees along the railroad track. From time to time, someone would hear a rustling noise among the kudzu vines and exclaim, "There he goes! I saw the monkey!" But when pressed for a description, the story never matched up with any of the sightings before that one.

Buzz, however, was a true believer. He'd made up the song about the monkey magically appearing on Christmas Eve and bringing presents to children everywhere. Shelly had been singing it for the past week. I only had a few more hours to endure the ditty; when the holiday had passed, she would stop.

Across the street, the two men and a woman were coming out of the house. One man went to the trunk of the county social-services car they had arrived in. He pulled out two wooden planks, a hammer, and some nails. He brought them back to the front door of our house. The other man held the board while the first man nailed them over the doorjamb where they had forced open the front door with a pry bar.

The woman stood on the front steps and scanned the kudzu clumps across from the house. Her gaze stopped exactly on the spot where we hid.

I put a hand on Shelly's shoulder. "Shhhhh."

From the corner of my eye I saw Buzz raise the broken binoculars to his eyes.

"Is she saying anything to the men?" I whispered.

Buzz said nothing but kept watching. Everything around us seemed to slow down as I waited for him to reply. A brown leaf, once shining in the Mississippi brightness, dropped from the branches above. It spiraled down past my head, and as it did, I saw it in microscopic detail: the curl of the crumble-thin edges, the veins now flat and empty, the pocked stem twirling, swirling down. The leaf brushed my cheek on its journey to the dirt.

I realized I was half-crouched, ready to run, my hand gripping Shelly's arm.

"Oww," she said. Her pointing arm was still slowly waving.

Buzz spoke. "She's telling them something."

As the woman spoke words we couldn't hear, the men turned away from the front door of our house. They looked directly at where we were hiding.

"The guy with the hammer is saying something now," said Buzz.

The train horn split apart the universe.

The two men on our porch both looked to their left. They started jogging across the yard toward us.

"Ben—" Buzz said. He had dropped the binoculars in the dirt.

"They can't see us," I said.

Shelly continued her pointing and waving.

The train blasted again.

The men were running now, crossing the street next to the tracks.

"Get ready," I said.

The men were sprinting. Their eyes were visible to us now, their faces grim and official.

Then all other sight and sound was obliterated.

The train horn roared as the clattering wall of boxcars blasted past us, only twenty feet away.

I clamped my hands over Shelly's ears. The assault of noise pierced my skull for a half-second, and then the locomotive charged beyond us. The rest of the train began rattling past us. The branches around us quivered as the train threw waves of winter wind against our natural fortress.

Buzz crouched at the side of the natural tent next to the opening where we crawled in and out, his hands over his ears.

Light and dark flashed at us rapidly as the train cars rushed by. Like a flickering movie reel, the spaces between the boxcars revealed the two men standing on the other side of the train. They waited for a moment but the train kept coming.

I looked at Buzz. He was out of his crouch and watching the train go by. His lips were moving, but I could hear no words. I realized he was counting the cars.

The men finally turned and walked away, their pace cut into tiny jerking steps by the interruption of the train.

Shelly took her hands from her ears and resumed her arm-sweeping scan of the branches above us. Her lips were moving and I knew she was singing the monkey song that Buzz had made up.

Across the street, the trio of social workers got into their car, backed out of the driveway, and drove away.

The train droned on. I glanced at Buzz. Without turning toward me, he shouted, "Hundred and eighty-seven!" loud enough to be heard above the track clatter.

I sank to the dirt floor of our hideout next to Shelly. My hands were jammed into the pockets of the stained corduroy coat that the church ladies had dropped off to our mother back in the summer. I remember thinking how I would never wear the ratty thing in public. With the rare advent of a snowy Christmas in Mississippi, I was glad I had the coat now.

My hand felt the crinkling of paper in the coat pocket. I pulled out the piece of ruled school paper and unfolded it. The regularity of the train's clack-clacking wheels lulled me into a false sense of security for a moment. I wanted to read the note again.

The date at the top of the page was October 23, 1967. I had written it using the pen I'd received from my grandmother the previous Christmas. The pen was in my other pocket, the only possession I'd taken from our house before we had rushed out the back door and looped back through the neighborhood to our hideout.

The rest of the writing on the sheet of paper was from our mother, who had apparently grabbed one of Shelly's number one pencils and stabbed out the note while we were at school that fall day.

The note was only a few sentences long. I had read the message a dozen times before, not just in this note but on other notes at other places in other times. "Benjy, watch the other two while I am gone. I got to find Barry before it gets too late. You keep them out of trouble. You know your Mama loves you. Won't be long.—Mama."

I folded the note and put it back into my pocket. When I glanced over at Buzz, he was watching me carefully.

The caboose whooshed past, and the clattering faded away from us.

The quietness was eerie now. Buzz still stared at me, and I realized he was searching for any sign of sadness or panic. Satisfied at not finding any, he kneeled in the dirt and picked up the binoculars again.

His voice seemed to boom when he spoke. "She's not coming back."

It wasn't a question.

In my peripheral vision I saw Shelly's head jerk slightly, but she pulled it back quickly and continued her monkey-searching sweep. She was humming the song louder now.

I looked at Buzz. "Don't say that."

"You know it's true. Why shouldn't I say it?" His voice was lower now, almost hissing.

I cut my eyes toward our sister and gave Buzz my best silencing stare.

He ignored the warning. "How do you know she really is coming back this time?"

His face remained stonelike, but his eyes were shiny now.

I had not even realized when I put my hand on Shelly's shoulder. I felt her convulse as her little song was interrupted by a sob. I knelt and put my arms around her and squeezed my eyes shut. We felt our brother's hands on us even before we heard him move.

"I'm sorry," he whispered.

We sat, listening to the wind curl through the kudzu branches all around us. The sun had set, and the dusk was falling on us rapidly. The first few flakes of snow began to fall, just as the astounded TV weatherman had forecast.

But at least we had each other.

It was at that moment, however, as we clenched and drained one another of any balm of comfort we could get, that we heard the noise. A rustling in the branches above us tilted our noses skyward. At first we didn't see him. Then Shelly slowly raised her arm and pointed. "He is here."

He was backlit by the street lamp that blinked on just at that moment. But we could see him.

"He really came," Buzz murmured, amazed.

The silver flakes gave a frosting to our canopy of vines as the Christmas monkey brought a dash of wonder to our dismal evening. He remained for a moment, watching us, as if he wished he had a gift to leave us.

And, for that time and place, it was enough.

"So," my daughter says, "once again you've driven six hours just to stare at your childhood home for a few moments."

Her voice brings me halfway back from that moment on Christmas Eve that was the lowest in my memory. Even before we learned that our mother would never return, just as Buzz had predicted—and before the foster homes and our escapes, before the orphanage, and before our eventual graduations and producing families of our own—that huddled pooling of our sadness evokes a desperation in me, albeit temporary, after all this while. I can still vividly see those children, heartbroken and abandoned, in my mind's eye.

"You know, I asked Uncle Buzz and Aunt Shelly about it," she says. "And they say the same thing you did. Your mom died here and left the three of you to survive on your own."

I turn to her. "That is true, sweetie."

Her face brims with the kind of skepticism that only a college freshman can produce. If it were possible for her to psychically peel away the fortress that is my mind and yank the truth from me, she would. But I just smile pleasantly until the intensity she inherited from her mother and grandmother drains away and is replaced with a smirk.

"Okay, old man," she says, "if you say so."

We stand side by side for a few seconds longer and face the house across the street on the other side of the tracks. Even though the weather is above freezing, someone in a happy house nearby has lit a fire. The faint scent of coziness crosses my senses as the hard wood burns.

Miles away a train drones. We both turn in the direction of the sound but see nothing. It is far away.

We step over the rails and lava rock and weathered ties and move toward the car.

I open her door for her, as I've done since the day she was born. Above our heads, the grayness of the December day begins to lighten.

I close my door and turn the key. "Ready for a nice meal in the Quarter?"

She gives me a true smile, the one that makes everything worthwhile. "Guess I'll do anything for a real muffaletta."

As I ease back out onto the street, I watch her as she strokes the small smooth monkey once again.

Queen Elizabeth Running Free

by Ruth Campbell Williams

You never know in Mississippi. About Christmas weather, that is. One year it's sleeting and freezing. Next it's hot enough to make tar run. Today it was rainy. Windy. Cold. It made my bed cozy and me lazy.

Jake was up in bed with me, adding to the coziness, and we stayed there until well past nine. It was pleasant, and when I couldn't doze anymore, I propped myself on pillows and enjoyed looking at my doll.

Seems strange even to me that a woman well past fifty keeps a doll on her bureau, but Miss Elizabeth has been with me for most of those fifty years, and there's too much wrapped up in her by now to think of putting her away. Like this morning when I lay there, I wasn't so much thinking of her gold dress or the blue royalty sash she wears from shoulder to hip. It was more of a daydream about my daddy.

It was Daddy who gave her to me, on a Christmas morning in the 1950s. He'd been all the way to Memphis to find her, to a fancy toy store that sold Madame Alexander dolls. And he'd carried a picture with him that I'd been mooning over for months.

The Queen Elizabeth doll was my first real dream, and good daddies live to make their daughter's dreams come true.

Even today, when Daddy is long dead and most of my dreams have been shrunk to about the size of a dime, Miss Elizabeth provokes me into smiling. What joy I had that Christmas! Daddy had done himself proud in other ways, as Santa, and we two girls (my sister, Leslie, and me) were hysterical with excitement. There was a whirly jig, just like the one in the schoolyard, and a roller coaster about twelve feet high from top to bottom with a small rickety cart that was only big enough for one child at a time. We screamed and screamed, clattering to the bottom in the cart. And I lay in bed today with my arms wrapped tight around me, remembering the terror and thrilling fun of it.

All that is in Miss Elizabeth. Along with Daddy's secret wink to Momma and his big smile when he handed me the box, such a long box with a floppy pink bow on top. Tissue paper rustled as I lifted the lid. Momma giggled. Daddy drew hard on his cigarette. When I saw Queen Elizabeth, I couldn't help gasping. My hands shook with lifting her, I was being so careful of disturbing her. She was royalty, even in our cluttered den, with her rhinestone tiara, rich lame gown, every detail perfect, right to her ruffled gold satin underpants and flesh-toned nylons. There was a blue garter on one leg. But it took me long minutes to discover all these things, hours even. That day was so fine that it can still light up a Christmas morning just through remembering.

As I lay in bed this morning, staring at Queen Elizabeth, I began to weep for Momma and Daddy and for the old and gone times in this very house, my house now. Modernized and comfortable with central heat and air. But not the bustling home of my childhood. Then I thought of Leslie and how I'd be seeing her later on and that cheered me.

I was dabbing at my eyes with the hem of the sheet when the phone started ringing. Jake barked after every ring so it was a regular cacophony. I tried to ignore it. I fluffed the pillow and burrowed under the covers and closed my eyes. Christmas morning, I said out loud.

But the horrible noise kept on. Hammer on glass followed by the thunder of deep-throated barking.

Thirty-one times that phone jangled. I counted every one of them, thinking it would be the last. But on it went. Thirty-one times. I never wanted a phone to shut up so much as I did this morning.

It was thirty-six times before I got up, helped Jake out of bed, and bundled myself in my fuzzy robe. I walked fast as I could into the kitchen, but I took a minute to stare at the caller ID before I answered.

William Everett III. A hoity name for a man who's nothing like a gentleman, despite the fact that he's a third and his daddy was nice and as sweet a man as I ever met.

My name's Everett, too. Mrs. Everett, the preacher calls me. But everyone else knows me by my first name. Wimsy.

I know I should have gotten rid of the Everett when I got rid of William, only by then all my documentation was tied up with the Everett, and it was a lot of trouble to change it. I kept it out of practicality.

I snatched that phone up, some angry but mostly startled when I saw William's name on the ID box. I pinched the throat of the receiver between two fingers like it might coil itself around and fang me. Sure enough that old forked tongue was on the other end.

"Wimsy?" it said. "This is William." He announced himself like he was a prize.

"What?"

"Merry Christmas," he said. He sounded pouty, maybe hurt I wasn't more glad.

"Why are you calling me, William?" I didn't say after twenty years. I thought that went without saying. But he spoke up like we'd never been apart all those years. Divorced. Me shed of him, and him with that Slatey woman who'd had him now ever since.

I don't mind her having him. I never had. It was Slatey who got me into the divorcing frame of mind in the first place. The night I found out about her, I lay awake with happy feelings, relief mostly, that he was on her and not on me, and for the first time I felt glad that William and I didn't have kids.

Slatey did me a favor. Maybe did him one too, if she could love him better than me. Because by then I'd quit loving William.

I'd loved him once though, hard and constant and relentlessly no matter what. You'd think after sixteen years of such deep loving it'd take a big wrong to kill the feeling. But it didn't. It was a small thing compared to some others.

I said, I'll drive. You're drunk. And he pushed me up against the car, holding me there with one hand flat against my chest. He leaned down in my face—the smell of liquor breath made me want to vomit—and he spit on me, right in the eyes. Spit burns in an eye, or maybe it was the liquor, and it made me yelp and jerk away from him.

It was that moment, exactly, when love stopped. It rolled itself up like a window shade. Pffft.

I left our crummy rental house the morning after I found out about Slatey and walked to the bus station. It was a hot midsummer day, dusty and dry, and I wore the scantiest decent dress I had. Dotted swiss, with an empire waist and no sleeves. The only things I took were Queen Elizabeth, cradled in my arms, and a cracked fake leather purse hooked in my elbow. I rode fourteen hours from Houston, Texas, to Tutwiler, Mississippi, to Daddy's house. Me and Queen Elizabeth, running free.

"I miss you," William said on the phone this morning. "I never stopped loving you."

"You drunk?"

"I only had a few."

"I'm hanging up."

"It's Christmas. Can't you talk to me, baby?"

His voice was cracking, trembly when he said baby.

"What do you want William?" I felt a little wistful after he said baby. It's been a long time since anyone's called me baby. It reminded me of the way he was when we were young. I was only eighteen when we married. He was twenty, so tall and big shouldered and handsome I could have spent all my time looking at him, let alone touching on him. He was that fine a built man, and he moved like a flow of water, smooth enough to make you cry with the beauty of it.

"I was thinking this morning of how you used to sit on the toilet lid and prop a leg up on the tub," he said.

"What are you going on about?"

He snorted, sounded exasperated. "How you used to shave your legs baby."

"Oh."

"I was thinking how sexy you were when you did it. How long your legs were. How pretty your hands were."

I never knew he watched me like that. I always thought I was lucky to have him and he'd settled for me. I smiled in spite of myself, to hear he missed me for my looks, of all things.

"Slatey isn't going to like hearing you talk to me about it," I said. I was trying real hard to pull back from him. William isn't a man you want to give a hitch of hope to. He'd wrap you up in it so fast that you'd be caught before you could turn your head to run. It scared me that I'd even be in the position to be caught when I'd thought all this time I was free.

"Slatey's not here," he said.

"Where is she?"

"She's gone. Or rather I'm gone from her. She kicked me out." He sounded full of self pity. "Least you had enough kindness to leave me with a place to live," he said.

I heard a clink of glass against the phone. The sound of liquid going down his gullet. Hang up, I said to myself.

"You O.K.?" My face burned with shame that he'd already wheedled me into feeling sorry for him.

"I'm getting by. Thanks for asking."

His voice was matter of fact when he said it. Thanks for asking. Him inviting me to ask some more things. But I was regretting asking the first thing. I was looking around my kitchen. Seeing how clean and shiny it is. Admiring my new café curtains. Wanting to be alone to enjoy them. I looked at the coffee pot and wished I'd pushed the button before I answered the phone. I wished I'd gone to the bathroom.

I got aware of myself and brushed a hair out of my eyes. Realized it wasn't a hair, but a tear.

The rain was drumming, and I looked up at the ceiling. It was loud, too loud. It didn't feel cozy anymore. What it felt was gloomy and dark. Scary. I reached down and pulled Jake over next to my leg. He licked my hand.

"Where are you?" I asked.

"I got me a used RV, baby. All my stuff's in it."

"You mean your books?" I said. That's all he'd ever owned. Books.

You'd think he'd learn something from them, but that was the riddle of William. How smart he was, how much he knew, how little it helped him to be a good person. I know the empty truth of him, that his brain is full of words but his soul is a wretched lost thing.

I had reached the button on the coffee pot by then, and I watched it start to drip. I was listening hard to find out where William was in his RV.

"Yeah. It's me and my books. *On the road again,*" he sang. "Remember us being on the road, baby?"

He was sounding dreamy, happy, drunk. "Hell yeah, I remember," I said, so angry with him and scared of him that my heart was beating full in my ears. "I remember getting ripped off in Miami, arrested for vagrancy in Atlanta. You remember getting beat up outside a bar in West Texas? You remember that?"

"Jesus! No need to yell." He sniffed. "It's just like you to remember the bad stuff. Can't you remember the rest of it?" He said, calm like he was a hypnotist, rocking a shiny object in front of me, "Remember the good stuff, Wimsy. Try."

"There wasn't any good stuff," I said. "Except in the beginning, when we were still at home here in Tutwiler."

"Tutwiler." He sounded disgusted when he said the word. He had hated that quiet life. He had wanted more than anything to get away, and back then I'd do anything he wanted.

"That's where I was happy," I said. "The rest is like a bad dream to me now."

"Shoot, Wimsy. You're not trying," he said. "Remember San Onofre Beach? Remember we drank three bottles of California Merlot, and made love, and watched the sun come up?"

"Yeah," I said. "And I remember being sick to my stomach and finding out you lost the car keys, and we only had twenty dollars. And you running away with your surfboard into the ocean while I figured out how to break into the car. Yeah, I remember San Onofre."

"How'd you get so angry? You used to be such a soft, sweet girl. Remember how broke we were our first Christmas in Texas, how you made flowers out of toilet paper for tree ornaments? I still think that was the nicest tree we ever had."

That's when I hung up. It flew all over me for him to mention my paper flowers. To make me pitiful for having tried so hard all those years ago to make our life prettier and him not trying at all, or even knowing how to try.

I punched the buttons on the ID box and deleted his name and phone number. I kept deleting till the readout said No Calls. I wished life was that way. Delete, delete, delete.

I went outside then, no umbrella or even any shoes. I walked up my driveway, hardly feeling the pea gravel. When I got under the cottonwood tree at the creek, the wind blew and shivered me all over with pent-up raindrops. I ran from there to the wooden gate at the end of the drive and latched it. The padlock was rusty and almost never used, but I pounded it together with my bare hand until my whole arm was throbbing and it was locked and I was safe.

All I could think was that an RV might be coming any minute. Might be just over the hill. And I had to keep it out so I could be warm and cozy in my kitchen. A cup of coffee. My dog. My Christmas Day the way I had planned it, with no calls and no RV parked in my yard.

Around noon the phone rang again. I checked the ID before I answered. For an instant, I swear, it said William Everett. Then I blinked, and the letters spelled out Leslie Johnson. "'Lo?" I said, a little shaky from the experience of having a hallucination.

"We're here," Leslie said. "Why's the gate locked?"

"Long story," I said.

The rain had stopped but the sky was still overcast and the wind fresh with another cold front moving in. I pulled on a jacket and walked up the drive. When I got the gate open, Leslie drove her black Silverado past me. I waved at the three girls inside. They were tumbling here and there over the seats, and I could hear their squeals. I locked the gate and walked to the truck to say hello.

The window went down and my big sister stuck her head out, every gray hair colored blond, so that she looked a bit like a flaxen-haired child. Or maybe it was the excitement of Christmas morning that made her so young looking. "Merry Christmas," she said. Her face was rosy cheeked. Her eyes sparkling. She glanced over the seat at the girls. "Santa brought everyone a new Barbie," she said.

"Oh my," I said. I opened the back door and slid in next to Cassie, the youngest.

"Can we play with Queen Elizabeth?" She asked right away, her eyes round with knowing how seductive she is, how pretty, how completely lovable.

"I'll put her on the card table so your Barbies can meet her," I said, frowning so she'd know I wasn't a pushover. "But no one can touch her. O.K.?"

Cassie nodded, solemn. I looked around at the other two girls, Imsy the middle child—named after me but pronounced without the *W* because she couldn't say it when she started talking—and Les, the oldest. They were Leslie's grandchildren.

I served everyone a slice of pound cake with strawberries and whipped cream, and we all sat around the kitchen table to eat it. Leslie and I had eggnog with ours, like Daddy used to make, from scratch with plenty of Bourbon. I lit the tall red Christmas candle and put it in the center of the table before I sat down. It looked very festive.

The conversation was all about Barbies and their clothes. Aunt Wimsy, did you see this dress? Grandma Les does this outfit match? Leslie and I could hardly eat our pound cake for all the looking at and inspecting we had to do. But every so often I'd see her watching me, and when she saw me see her, Leslie'd raise an eyebrow, and I knew she was wondering about the gate.

"Leave Aunt Wimsy and me alone," she said finally. "Queen

Elizabeth is waiting over there to hold court." She motioned to the card table and the girls ran off, leaving piles of Barbie clothes and shoes and hats scattered around the table. I began to put them away, enjoying the sparked up memories of holding doll things again, but pretending to be doing a chore so I didn't have to look at Les. I didn't want to talk about William. I already knew her opinion of him, and I was still feeling ashamed that after all this time he'd gotten to me.

"Law," I said to Leslie, "what a mess." The old-fashioned sound of my words reminded me of my grandmother. Leslie draped an arm over my shoulders, so I knew it reminded her, too. She was watching her granddaughters--three perfectly darling children, making believe with their dolls--and her arm around me made me part of it, so I was happy and sad at once, knowing that precious few of these moments come to us. There are none to spare. Time moves so fast. I glanced quickly at Queen Elizabeth and could feel tears coming on.

I sat up, and Leslie's arm fell away.

"I'm thinking of building a trellis for my Lady Banks," I said to her.

"Oh, you and your projects," Leslie said. "You're always doing something to this place. Makes me ashamed of my own yard." Then she stood and collected the dishes and carried them to the sink. When she sat down again her face was dead serious. She patted my hand so I'd look at her. "Are you O.K., Wimsy? Why was the gate locked?"

I smiled and squeezed her hand. "I'm O.K.," I said.

She peered at me, and I thought of her as she had once been, the graceful dancer, always the star of school recitals, and for an instant I missed that innocent girl. But I blinked the thought of missing away and thought instead of how good it was to be with this warm-hearted, pudgy grandmother. And I felt guilty for not telling her about William. So I hugged her instead. "Are you having a good Christmas?" I asked.

"The best," she said. "My grandkids keep me young."

She didn't mention her husband, Kenny, his bad health, his bad attitude. That's like her to always see the good in a situation. I looked over at the girls. Their chatter had quieted, and they were watching us, their mouths agape while they listened. Getting a peek at who we are besides Aunt Wimsy and Grandma Les must have startled them. They looked surprised. I turned toward the window. The sun had come out.

"William phoned this morning," I said. It popped out.

Leslie's chair legs squeaked against the wood floor. "No," she said. Her eyes were sick looking, peaked and angry at once.

"That's why I had the gate locked."

"What did he want?" She balled a fist in her lap, and I began to feel sorry for making her so upset.

"He was drunk. Lonely. Slatey kicked him out."

"Where is he?"

"I don't know. He might be anywhere. He's living in an RV."

"Well, he's not your problem anymore," Leslie said. Then she added, "Is he?"

My stomach flipped over. Could she see that weakness in me? I pictured it. William in my life again, in my house, in my bed. I rubbed my palm back and forth on the cherry table. I could feel Leslie's anxiety grow as the seconds ticked on and I didn't answer her.

Then I slapped my hand down hard. It hurt so bad my eyes watered and I curled my fingers around the pain. The hurt William had done me was because I'd let him, like I'd been hurting myself with my own hands. It flashed on me that I'd had a sickness.

"Wimsy?" Les said.

"Let's not spoil Christmas," I said. I reached over and touched her cheek and bit my lip, hoping she'd leave me alone.

Leslie laid her hand over mine against her cheek. "You're not going to let him manipulate you, are you?" she said, holding my hand so tight I couldn't pull free. I blinked a few times. For some reason I thought of Daddy's eyes when he'd handed me the box with Elizabeth in it. He wasn't expecting anything but my happiness from that gift. Then I thought of William saying he still loved me, and I looked at Leslie straight on.

"William's lost the battle," I said. "I don't want him." I know Leslie thought I meant William had lost me. She nodded and let go of my hand. But what I really meant was that William had lost the battle to know how to love. In a way it made me feel that he had died.

I looked at the girls, whispering and watching me, and was embarrassed that I'd made such a scene by slapping my hand on the table. I ducked my head and walked to the sink to do the dishes.

When the kitchen was tidy, Leslie and I went into the living room and called the girls to come open presents. My Christmas tree was floating on a mountain of gifts, and I had several more hidden in the sideboard.

"Wimsy, this is too much," Leslie said. "You spoil them."

"It's only once a year."

Leslie went to the truck and came back with a big box for me, a collection of jigsaw puzzles and some books. And I gave her a dozen jars of preserves and a nightgown.

She and I opened our gifts quietly. Imsy and Little Les and Cassie tore into theirs with high-pitched shrieks. Boxes and bows and paper piled up around them, and Leslie got up to try and control the chaos. She circled the room with a garbage bag.

Queen Elizabeth stood forgotten on the card table by the fireplace, looking serene and free of care. I walked over and made a fuss of straightening her skirt, which didn't need straightening. She was perfect as she'd always been.

I added a log to the fire and replaced the screen. On my way back to the sofa I bent down and retrieved a piece of yellow tissue from the litter. By the time all the gifts were opened, I had made a paper flower and put it behind my ear.

Blue's Holiday

by Jacqueline F. Wheelock

Christmas Eve, 1966

Lavender Blue was an even five feet. So it was mostly head, neck, and hands that the guests saw, if one of them happened to notice her, laboring behind a loaded cleaning cart, up and down the lofty hallways of the Biloxi Chateau. It was Christmas Eve, and Blue (that's what everyone called her) had just finished cleaning the rooms assigned to her on the beach side of the fourth floor when the familiar images from her past, which she had managed to suppress all morning, appeared atop the cart in front of her like a bubbling bowl of rapidly spoiling soup—Memory Soup, from which she had, with delight, secretly tasted for years—now beginning to leave a rancid, questioning taste in her mouth. She closed the door to the last room that looked out onto the Gulf and struggled to make the cart turn toward the row of rooms on the back side, hoping and praying that just the movement itself would topple the memories from the cart of her mind.

Blue thought to herself: *At twenty years old, my mind ought to be as sharp as a pocket knife, separatin' truth from lies.* But the dish that memory served her this morning was choked with bits of old, mysterious ingredients—not mysterious in the sense that she could no longer make out the details, but mysterious because she had become more and more convinced that *none of these here things ain't never happened!* Things like little brown and black and yellow faces, turned upward toward a bright red fire engine. And rainbows of cellophane-wrapped candies on a winter wind, streaming down from the red truck like big-city confetti. And squashed black ears, peeping out from behind a beard that had the whiteness of a miniature cotton field. *This here just don't make no sense. I swear it don't!*

That last memory—the one about the ears and the cotton—was the silliest, most unlikely of all because practically all the cotton fields in Mississippi were inland, and she had never been any further from the Mississippi Gulf Coast than Mobile to the east of Biloxi and New Orleans to the west. And while it was true that Blue had at least *seen* fire engines and cellophane wrappers in her time, she couldn't recall ever even glimpsing a field of cotton except in a magazine. Yet in all her craziness, it was that ears-and-cotton memory that wooed (and troubled) her the most, especially this time of year.

She stopped the cart in front of a room that happened to display a "Do Not Disturb" tag on its door. Leaning her forehead on the cart's handle, she closed her eyes to see if she could force out of her head all the pictures that troubled her and hold fast to the few that did not. She would rest a minute before she moved on to call out her interminable "Housekeeping!" announcement.

Then she remembered the Christmas music she had purchased. She squeezed her earlobe to start up the gigantic singing earring shaped in the form of bells that she had bought from a temporary holiday stand along the beach yesterday. It seemed louder than when she had played it in the privacy of her duplex this morning. *I hope this don't wake up the guests.* For a moment, blessed relief settled upon her, simply from stopping the cart if nothing else, because along with the uninvited mind storm she was encountering this morning, she had gotten stuck with the one cart in the hotel with a wobbly wheel—cl-CLACK, cl-CLACK, cl-CLACK, cl-CLACK. So if she could conquer nothing else in this stolen respite, just bringing that fiendish cart noise to a halt and resting her senses with a bit of holiday music from the oversized earring—without Housekeeping finding out—would be a minor coup.

But wait a minute. I don't hear no music no more!

Suddenly her music had stopped. With her eyes still closed, she reached to her earlobe again to be sure she had not somehow knocked the gaudy music maker onto the carpet. The earring was still there, but it no longer responded to her touch. *Out of whack, I reckon. Just like everything else. Done prob'ly caught the contrary spirit of this here cart.* She permitted herself a faint smile at her own wittiness. Then, almost mindlessly, she opened her eyes, lifted her head, and glanced across the hall through the open door of a guest room she had cleaned a little while ago on the beach side of the hotel. Through the window, out across U. S. Highway 90, she could see that the fog had lifted, and the string of Christmas lights on the other side of the highway, which had looked like colored pearls at 7:00 a.m., now, at ten o'clock, glared down garishly at the sand like the cheap electric lights they really were. *Fake and ugly, just like these here earrings I'm wearin', just like these here crazy memories is gettin' to be, just like what I keep on doin' back in that room of mine. Everything 'bout my life been either ugly or fake. 'Cept for the loneliness. It's just as real and terrible and endless as that water on the other side of them lights.*

Two nights ago, in her boarding room near the Back Bay, Blue had begun her secret yearly ritual of fighting loneliness by dressing up in a red Santa suit she had found in back of the hotel when she was sixteen, lighting what remained of the one red candle she owned, and crying until no sweat or spit, let alone tears, remained in her body. She had never known it, but she was a pretty girl in a haunting, heart-wrenching kind of way, tiny and jet black with enormous eyes and perpetually raised brows that spoke of indelible shock. But for all her delicate looks, life had hardened her, so that she was often off-putting and defensive to the casual observer. Once in a great while, she might indulge herself with some trinket—a necklace or a bracelet perhaps—hoping that she would appear a bit softer to any soul who might take the time to look. But that was as far as her attempt at attractiveness went, especially when it came down to body ornaments. Never before had she adorned her ears, because her classmates in elementary school always said she had "pinned-back rabbit ears." But yesterday, thinking she might revive the cheer of her yearly ritual gone sour, she had dared to buy earrings, red and dangling, marketed as Jingle Bells. And though one of them was destined never to work, for the last twelve hours or so, the one that did work had been caroling her on demand until, just minutes ago, it abruptly quit—jinxed by the wobbly cart.

She had arrived at work this morning feeling a touch of excitement because of the holiday earrings, when a tall, caramel-colored shapely maid happened to notice them—just as the working one mysteriously started to play "Jingle Bell Rock" on its own. The girl, who had never even nodded at Blue before, decided to address her in a partly complimentary, partly condescending manner in front of all the workers collecting their equipment and supplies from Housekeeping at the shift change.

"Aw shucks, now! Look at cha, now! Tryin' to git on the beam, huh? With them li'l singin' earrings on them li'l squashed-down ears! Aw shucky ducky, now! Look at chu!"

Blue quickly jerked her head down to her chest, and the music stopped, leaving behind the dangling earrings themselves to make a tinny sound out in the middle of the silence. But when she raised her head again to the sound of delayed laughter, all traces of hope and congeniality with which she had begun the day were gone from her face. She had wanted simply to be noticed, not advertised. In defiance and amidst the guffawing, she had decided against removal of her earrings, and observing that the only cart left was the wobbly one, she loaded it and quickly left the room.

The hardening of Blue was tied to the fact that she had lost two mothers in as many years and had never known a father. Indeed, that her father had ever stood on the earth's surface seemed never to have mattered to anyone, especially to her long-deceased second mother who had reared her in the country thirty-five miles northeast of Biloxi—the one she had called Uttermutter. And her birth mother, who died when she was fifteen, hardly mattered either because Blue had never even seen her. But unlike in the case of her father, when Blue was a child growing up in the country, she had at least gathered whisperings of her mother's past.

What she had gathered was that her mother had been a part-time palm reader from Louisiana who wouldn't—or couldn't—handle a tenth bastard child. But although her mother had believed one more child an ugly, impossible thing to bear, still she loved pretty names, so Blue had been told. So the palm reader called the last child she would ever give birth to Lavender Blue after an old rhyme she had heard once upon a time when she was growing up in Algiers. She gave her the gift of a beautiful name. Then she gave her away when she was three days old and fled to Florida with the remaining nine, convincing on the spot a selfish cousin named Tangerine, by looking at her palms, that Blue would bring a mysterious boon to her in her old age if she could just find it in her heart to rescue her right then and be her other mother.

"Now, listen, Cousin Tangy," said Blue's mother in her voodoo voice, randomly adding a jazzy New Orleans "yeah" and "no" at the end of her pronouncements. "This ain't no ordinary child here, *no.* She go'n be able to see things down the road—things that's sho go'n help you. You don't know it yet, but you go'n be needin' a mighty lot o' help, *yeah*—when you git old, you know. The only reason I moved up here to the country in the f'ust place was to be a help to you, givin' you free readins when you be needin' 'em."

Cousin Tangy muttered under her breath. "Only reason you here is to chase after other folks' mens. That's how come you here. I knows it, and you know it, too."

"Like I said," continued Blue's mother, ignoring her cousin's tone, "ain't I done helped you lots o' times with my readins when you needed it, *yeah?*"

Cousin Tangy, half wondering why Blue's mother could never improve her own lot with the readings, reluctantly took the child, partly out of the possibility that she truly might make her a servant of sorts one day and partly out of fear of voodoo reprisal. And she probably never would have kept her as long as she did but for the lucrative surprise that came in the mail when Blue was nearly three. She had always taught the child to call her Cousin Tangy, but after the money started to come in,

Tangy started to refer to herself as the child's "other mother."

"Just remember, I'm yo' other mother long as I'm on this earth. Just you remember that: yo' other mother."

So baby Blue who could not pronounce "other mother" started to call her Cousin Tangy Uttermutter.

Blue. What a name for a black girl, she used to think when she grew older. But working for white folks later in life taught her that "black and blue" was really one word, one concept. "Hon, he beat her 'til she was blacknblue," she would hear them say. Or "When I woke up the mornin' after that nasty fall I took, why, I was completely blacknblue!" So she guessed it must have been conceivable, if not desirable, for her to be black—and Blue, too.

She had pushed the rickety cart a foot or two further up the hall when she realized that the open door to the room across the hall was showing more than just the string of Christmas lights on the beach. She stopped the cart again and strained to pull it backwards. There was a man in there—a black man, sitting in the lounging area of the suite at a table facing the beach. *Where he come from? He must'a snuck in there while I was cleanin' another room!* She could not see his eyes because his back was turned to her, but his shoulders spoke of deep-seated dignity and defiance. There had certainly been no one in the suite when she cleaned it earlier, and there had been nothing to indicate that the guest was black. She had noticed that there had been no hair in the combs or wastebaskets or the basin. No cosmetics. No magazines. Nothing that spoke of whom the person was, and she had thought that odd. But standing here looking at him now, Blue entertained no question about his blackness, for the color of his neck, his ears—even his haircut—was unmistakably black. *Maybe he just now checkin' in. Naw! The Chateau don't be lettin' nobody in 'fo noon, and anyhow, there was a robe hanging behind the bathroom door.* This man, whoever he was, had seemingly gone out of his way to be out when it was cleaning time and to make sure that maid service noticed nothing unusual about him. But now the door was swung wide open for all the world to see.

This was only the third time Blue had seen one of her own race as a guest in the hotel, and it unnerved her. A lot had happened in the several years since Dr. Gilbert Mason had led the wade-in into the segregated waters of the Gulf of Mexico, unearthing friction between blacks and whites solid enough to spread on toast. But good things were happening, too. Many last bastions of supremacy, like the Biloxi Chateau, were being forced to loosen their grips. Even so, everybody knew that things were nowhere near settled between the races, and only a fool, if he was black, would sit with his back turned to an open door in the Biloxi Chateau. Though, as a whole, the management of the hotel wore a necessary suit of racial tolerance, there were still those working there who did not mind passing down the word through the lower ranks that an uppity colored man in a certain room might need to be dealt with after hours—just as long as the Biloxi Chateau didn't dirty its hands.

She sensed that the man could feel her eyes on his back and was about to turn toward her. Quickly, she tried to move from his view, but it was a second too late when she got the stubborn misaligned wheel to turn loose the carpet. The man had seen her, and she had seen him. She nodded nervously. Then cl-CLACK, cl-CLACK. The wheels moved on toward the rest of the rooms assigned to Lavender Blue on the backside of the hallway.

Six hours later, she stood in front of her rented room at a boarding house on the Back Bay anticipating the familiar loneliness waiting for her inside. When she moved in four years ago, no one had inquired about age because Blue was ageless. On any given day, she could be fifteen or she could be thirty-five, depending on the hardness of the shell she wore at the time. And the nostalgic ambience of "boarding house" as a description of Blue's place of residence had been and still was a misnomer—if not an outright lie—perpetrated by her landlord. What she lived in was no more than a tiny ramshackle clapboard duplex with matching stoops. It sat across the street from a row of larger duplexes, which were not in much better condition but they offered more room and were exclusively for whites. The landlord of this strip of tenements, who happened to also be the manager of the Chateau, was a severe, ambitious man who saw himself as a future modern-day robber baron providing necessary lodging for his hired help, but he was also quite religious. And though he prided himself on a certain amount of sympathy toward the Negro and his recent struggles, he still felt the Lord had meant for each kind to remain with its own. Cattle with cattle, monkeys with monkeys, and Negroes with Negroes. So he had placed his tenements, though on the same street, on different sides—for the sacred sake of separation. Just daring to place them on the same street was quite generous, he thought.

She opened the door of her side of the duplex to the smell of lingering wax and dim electric lights. Christmas Eve, and she had been at her annual ritual now for three days. She unbuttoned her uniform and let it fall to the floor, stepping out of it thinking, *for somebody who leaves ever'body else's rooms so clean, yours sho' look like hell, and where you git off forgittin' to turn off the lights? You can't keep up with yo' bills as it is!* But inside Blue's efficiency apartment, it was about neither cleanliness nor efficiency. It was about warfare against despair.

In the late forties when Blue was little, she lived in a small African-American community thirty-five miles northeast of Biloxi called the Settlement. Each December an anonymous white man would rent a fire engine and a driver, a Santa suit complete with white beard and black belt, and a wonderful set of noisemakers. Then on Christmas Eve, he would come rolling through the countryside, leaning over the edge of the truck, ho-ho-hoing and throwing out candy to the children. To Blue, the fire engine was a marvelous colossus of a red machine, featuring a giant of a man with a red face and red ears. All the children in the Settlement would run out to meet him, and for Blue, this annual event was only rivaled by the trimonthly visits of the county bookmobile. Santa Claus—red, white, and wonderful. Santa Claus—larger than life.

But starting when she was four, no sooner had the real Santa left the black neighborhood than another Santa appeared, not in a red truck but at Blue's door, always that very same day, dressed in full Santa regalia. Obviously a pillow stuffed into his pants, his bowl full of jelly was in total disharmony with the rest of his spare frame. He was short, skinny, and black, everything the real Santa was not. Blue knew he was a Negro because behind his cottony beard she could see his ears, small, slightly depressed at the top of the rise, and the color of Uttermutter's skillet. For some reason, she was able to overlook his black hands, nose, and cheeks but not his ears. Santa Claus had red ears, and there was no question about that. In all the years the black Santa came, Uttermutter never opened the door to him. *What he comin' roun' here for, she would say, lookin' crazy. It's jes like him to do somethin' crazy like this. Ever'body know Santa Claus is white. Always has been; always will be.* What she was *not* saying about his reason for coming would have been far more important to Blue had she been old enough to understand. But at the time what was said or unsaid about the man mattered little to her. She did not comprehend the audacity of what he was doing; she simply grew to love the short black Santa for the wonderment of it all. And, too, she loved him because, through the window pane, she saw and heard him singing, year after year, "Away in a manger, no crib for a bed," and something in his eyes said to her, "Black and Blue though you are, I care about you."

At the end of Blue's thirteenth year, her other mother's health began to fail, and the roles switched so that the rescued became the rescuer. Pieces of her—Blue the launderer, Blue the caregiver, Blue the babysitter, Blue the cook—were parceled out by Uttermutter to work for the rich folks on the beach in town. Catching rides with shipyard workers, fending off nasty advances, and giving up dreams of writing large children's books with glossy covers like the ones she had seen in the bookmobile, Blue forsook childhood for necessity. But over time and after the loss of Uttermutter, when she would occasionally reach back for just one pleasant memory, she would timidly say to the workers in a shrimp factory that she worked in at the time or in the veneer mill or in the kitchen of a restaurant, "Did y'all know that the real Santa Claus is a Negro?" and they would look at her and shake their heads and say, "Girl, don't you know nothin'? You jes as crazy as a road lizard." Loudly and nervously they would laugh and say, "You better not let them white folks hear you say that or you might jes end up swingin' from one of them live oaks." And so over time and through the pain, she thought that her memory and her mind had taken separate roads, and she was powerless to make them one again. *Do I truly remember him? Did he really happen?* When she found a Santa suit stuffed in a waste barrel behind the hotel one cold January evening in 1962, she decided to make the black Santa from her childhood come alive whether he ever really lived or not. She would have her own holiday every year from then on.

So on Christmas Eve of 1966, she stepped out of her uniform in the middle of the floor, went to the efficiency bed, which she never bothered to put back up into its recessed place in the wall anymore, and picked up the Santa suit. Exhausted from the usual day's work, she dragged her body into the pant legs, the hems already rolled three-fold, and took the single pillow from her bed and stuffed it into the waist. The jacket was missing three of its buttons, but the plastic belt still worked, so she tightened it almost to the point of pain. Settling the elastic band of the dingy beard around the base of her skull, she placed the musty red and white cap on her head. Then she lit the red candle and gingerly moved to the table in the kitchenette. She began to sing "Merry Christmas, Baby, You sho been good to me." *Too sad!* Suddenly, she snatched off the cap and undid her braids, so that each braid seemed to form its own fortress, separating itself into sentries of three. She flung her loose braids from side to side as she swayed to her own rendition of, "Jingle bell, jingle bell, jingle bell rock." Then she pulled in a breath, sighed, and began to softly hum:

Away in a manger, no crib for a bed,
The little Lord Jesus lay down his sweet head.
The stars in the bright sky looked down where he lay,
The little Lord Je. . .sus. . .

Abruptly, it seemed, all the music she had ever tried to muster and salvage from the totally discordant life that was hers had come to an end tonight in a dingy duplex on a back bay. Laying her head on the crook of her arm—much too close to the candle—she gave herself over to a torrent of tears.

The man in the room looked out the window at the sights of Christmas. Yesterday, he had taken a gamble, and he knew it. Although he did not have the profile of Martin or Medgar or even Gilbert Mason who was fighting so hard for the rights of black Biloxians, he was a behind-the-scenes civil-rights activist, and to those to whom it mattered, he was well known and recognized. But his life had been in jeopardy for so long that jeopardy had become a way of life.

When he was younger, all he could think about was becoming a singer. He would put Sinatra in his place someday, show him what real crooning was. He would woo with his voice like Nat King Cole. Nothing would get in his way, especially not the responsibility of a family and especially not a woman who already had enough children to start her own church, telling him that one of them was his. But when the child was three years old and he saw her for the first time, held high in somebody's arms squealing at the sight of a red fire engine, there had been no question in his mind but that she was his own. From then on, he had given money to her other mother out of whatever he earned. Even while he was in Korea, before he so much as bought himself a cupcake or a Coke, he sent money to little Blue. Foolishly, yesterday he thought she would recognize him, feel a connection that although perhaps injured, surely was not completely severed—could never be severed, at least in his own mind. He thought that if their eyes ever met again, somehow simple biology and history would blow open any barrier. But all she had done was nod, nod and run away like a scared rabbit—running from his blackness like everyone else in this hotel. He had to be in the delta tomorrow for yet another voter-registration drive, but it had taken him years to find her again. One more day, one more try. What could it hurt?

Christmas morning found Blue fast asleep in her red suit, next to a melted candle. She had dreamed of fields of cotton she'd seen advertised in the *Mississippi Farmer* magazine in the lobby of the Chateau. She pushed the beard away from her face and tested her legs. Wobbly but still working. After she had washed up, she stepped back into her uniform, which lay exactly where she'd left it. The hotel manager had announced to her yesterday, as though she did not know, that most Negroes did have families, so he had selected her to work on Christmas Day—because she did not.

When she got to work, a complaint was waiting for her. She must clean room 411 immediately because it was reported that it was never cleaned the day before. Her manager was visibly shaken—partly because of the rare complaint, but mostly because of the color of the complainer.

"Get it right this time, Blue."

"Yessir, but I did clean it. I'm pretty sure Housekeeping must'a checked after me like they always do . . ."

"Well, clean it again. I don't particularly appreciate complaints from the likes of him . . . well, anyway, just see about the room."

She rapped her knuckles against the mahogany wood on the door with aggravated urgency.

"Housekeeping!"

The door yielded to her knock, so quickly that for a moment Blue half wondered if someone had been waiting for the sound of her knock. Maybe it's a holiday elf, she quipped to herself, trying to push back her nervousness. But while the man behind the threshold was barely three inches taller than she, he was no elf. Indeed the figure who stood clutching the brass door knob was a man. And everything about him—shirt, trousers, tie—was impeccable and intriguing.

He stared at her, drinking from her countenance as though she were healing waters from a divine spring. Then his eyes landed on the red earrings. *Tasteless. Otherwise, she's not much changed—not much at all.* His hands were trembling, even the one that still rested on the doorknob. He must control himself, he thought. The old carol his mother had sung to him—and he had sung to Blue—"Away in a manger, no crib for a bed," welled up in his throat, but he forced it backward with a visible descent of his Adam's apple. This holiday season, the song had become a bittersweet maypole around which much of his faculties circled, dizzying him with what might have been. He wanted to reach out to her, swing her high in the air as the man had done before the fire truck years ago. Instead, he straightened his tie.

"Leave your cart in the hallway," he said. "Come in and close the door."

At first, Blue did not move. Obviously, he was used to giving orders. And, for that matter, she was used to taking them. *But not from him.* Furthermore, there was seduction in his voice, but she quickly conceded that it was not dirty. So she stepped inside—just barely.

"Excuse my manners," he said. "Good morning."

"Moanin'."

Now, he was examining her with his eyes, outright (and they both knew it) taking in every inch of her frame. She backed away.

"Oh, no, no," he said, "please. Please sit down. I won't hurt you. I promise."

Sit down? What's wrong with this man? Don't he see this uniform? "My boss said you wanted yo' room cleaned. I come to clean it—again."

"Please, please sit down." He took a few steps backward to ease the tension. "I—I guess you must see something—in my face—that's . . . that's troubling you—anger? If it is—anger, I mean—it's not toward you." He made a tent with his fingers and started to pace. "Let me see here. I had so hoped—How do I begin? Please, sit down. You can leave the door open if you're afraid of me."

Within a blink, she had slipped into her defensive mode.

"I ain't scared o' you. I ain't scared o' nobody. I just want to know what you want, is all. First, you almost make me lose my job—after

I cleaned yo' room good as I could. Then you git me up here and want me to sit down like some kind of guest."

"Why shouldn't I treat you like I would a guest?"

She laughed out loud.

"Mister, you got any idea how many white folks livin' rooms I done cleaned in my life and never sit down in a single one? This here yo' livin' room while you at the Chateau, and I'm yo' maid. I reckon I'll stand up 'til you git to the point."

"Listen," he said, sounding as though he would shake her if he dared, "listen to me. I'm as black as you are."

"Naw, you ain't. Not dressed and actin' like you is now, you ain't, and talkin' the way you do, you ain't."

"I took a chance for you yesterday. I'm taking a chance right now."

"You ain't took no chance for *me!* How you go'n be takin' chances for me when I don't even much know you?"

She doesn't know me. He took in a long breath through his nostrils and tried to calm himself. "Well, you see, it's like this. Although I have committed no crime, there are people right here in this hotel who, out of fear, see me as a wanted man. They're still fighting a war that has long since been over, and for them, capturing and perhaps even killing people like me is a trophy for a lost cause. I work for the rights of oppressed people, and I usually don't sit with the door open in a public place like this, not even up North. But I opened the door yesterday and sat with my back turned, hoping you would see me, hoping you would know . . ."

She remained perfectly still, but the room was starting to move. Halfway through a revolution, she realized that now *she* was studying *him,* indeed, staring at him. Lavender Blue was feeling intoxicated with the emerging recall of something seismic. But she remained in her spot.

"I don't know what you talkin' bout."

He went to one of the chairs at the table near the window and sat down facing her. He leaned forward and looked upward into her eyes.

"Have you ever been hungry?" he asked.

She said nothing in response to his inquiry about hunger. She figured her station in life spoke for itself.

"So hungry for worldly experience that you would do almost anything, go almost anywhere to get a taste of it?

He was speaking in riddles. She didn't have time for this. Her life had been too hard, too blunt, for riddles. But she would give him a few more minutes. She continued to listen.

"When I was your age, I was starving—for life, but I didn't know what life was. More than anything else I wanted to matter. Never mind that my skin color continually whispered to me of walls that couldn't be penetrated, societies that were permanently closed. I was determined that nothing was going to stop me. Nothing."

Still, she did not reply, but memory had begun inserting itself into her space as it had the day before, not in riddles, but in something as tangible as the glossy books of the old bookmobile and the . . .

the ears! I know them ears! The floor beneath her was definitely on an incline now as he continued to speak to her of hunger. She reached for the back of a chair to steady herself. But still she would not sit.

"Then one day I saw a little girl reaching out to a white Santa Claus on a fire truck, and a whisper crossed my soul. 'This is life; that little girl *is* life.'" His voice trembled.

Fire truck!

Blue drew a deep breath and gripped the chair tighter. Sometime very soon she was going to have to sit down or she would faint. She moved around and eased herself down to the edge of the chair, feeling as though she had violated a centuries-old code, crossed a line set in motion by cotton fields she had never seen. Deep-seated fear of history struck at the heart of her. She was not supposed to be sitting here, but what he had just said to her might just be her own history, such as it was, and sit she would for the hearing of it. She spoke through latticed fingers.

"It was you, wasn't it? Was it you? Oh, Lord Jesus, it was you! But why? Why did you have that kind of carin' for me? And why did you, when you was 'bout all I had to look forward to, just up and disappear?"

"The answer to both your questions is still *hunger*—the first was instinctual, the other misplaced."

"But I still ain't quite gittin' what chu sayin'. Why me? Why did you come to Uttermutter's house just to sing to me?"

He looked away from her for a moment.

"Serenading is not all I did for you, Blue . . ."

"You know my name?"

"Of course. I've always known your name. I found that out the first day I saw you near the fire engine."

"Well, then if you know my name, you must 'a knowed my real mama?"

"I knew her."

"Was my mama pretty?" Quickly, she turned her face from him. "I ain't pretty, you know."

"You're beautiful."

Blue had no idea how to respond to a pure compliment, so she didn't. Instead, she returned to her inquiry.

"You said, 'while ago, singing wasn't the only thing you did for me. What else did you do?"

"I sent money to Miss Tangy for you—until a few years ago. Didn't you get the money I sent?"

"Money! Naw! What money?"

The man looked stunned. "I sent money to your guardian for at least a decade."

She was having difficulty processing this. Uttermutter had always claimed abject poverty. All the times of hard work on the beach, all the factory work, and there had been *money* sent to her before Uttermutter's death that she could have put by?

"You still haven't told me why, if you cared so much, you just up and left."

"I 'up and left' because someone made me believe that home and my right to be here were not worth fighting for. In order to matter, I thought, I had to leave Mississippi. I was wrong. Nobody can change history, and no matter how many enemies I have here, the American South is my history. The so-called enemies I had in Korea were not my history, so when I left there, I left for good. But Mississippi is my history; I don't intend to ever leave again. Can you understand that?"

"I think so."

"All right then. So much for the leaving." He reached over and touched her ear, and she jumped back, setting off a round of "Rudolph the Red-Nosed Reindeer" from the gaudy earring that had decided to play again.

"Don't chu be touchin' my ears! Who told you that you could touch me?"

"I'm sorry," he said. "I was out of line."

Awkwardly, she removed the malfunctioning earrings. Then she looked at him, straight on.

"There's more to the carin' than just the singin' and the money, ain't it? I want to know more about the carin' part." Deep inside, she knew why he had touched her ears and she knew why he cared, but she wanted to hear him say it.

He cocked his head to the side and grinned boyishly, as though he were about to take a daring summer plunge into a murky creek.

"Well, now, the caring really started when I saw those ears of yours for the first time, squashed down like somebody had sat on them."

He ran his fingers across the tops of his own ears, and she squelched a giggle. There was something about the way he was teasing her that was warm and familiar, like the soft glow of the red candle back at the duplex, now burned to a stump. Could a man this caring have fathered a girl who was too tired from common labor to even tidy her own room—a girl that once slept in an alley in the French Quarter and was rescued from a rapist by a nun, a girl that couldn't quite make it through junior high because there was no address to give the principal, no proof that she was thirteen and not twenty-three? It couldn't be. It just could not be. But from the looks of things, it was. Now she was totally looking past the rest of him to his ears.

"You mean. . ."

She was unable to form the words, and he did not answer her. He simply smiled.

"Stay here a minute," he said, disappearing into the bedroom of the suite. When he returned, he was wearing the most ridiculous and wonderful Santa suit Blue had ever seen.

The Birds for Christmas

by Mark Richard

We wanted "The Birds" for Christmas. We had seen the commercials for it on the television donated thirdhand by the Merchant Seamen's and Sailors' Rest Home, a big black-and-white Zenith of cracked plastic and no knobs, a dime stuck in the channel selector. You could adjust the picture and have no sound, or hi-fi sound and no picture. We just wanted the picture. We wanted to see "The Birds."

The Old Head Nurse said not to get our hopes up. It was a "Late Show" after Lights Out the night before Christmas Eve. She said it would wake the babies and scare the Little Boys down on the far end of the ward. Besides, she said, she didn't think it was the type of movie we should be seeing Christmas week. She said she was certain there would be Rudolph and Frosty on. That would be more appropriate for us to watch on the night before Christmas Eve.

"*Fuck* Frosty," Michael Christian said to me. "I see that a *hunrett* times. I want to see "The Birds," man. I want to see those birds get all up *in* them people's hair. That's some real Christmas TV to me."

Michael Christian and I were some of the last Big Boys to be claimed for Christmas. We were certain someone would eventually come for us. We were not frightened yet. There were still some other Big Boys around—the Big Boy who ran away to a gas station every other night, the Human Skeleton who would bite you, and the guy locked away on the sun porch who the Young Doctors were taking apart an arm and a leg at a time.

The Young Doctors told Michael Christian that their Christmas gift to him would be that one day he would be able to do a split onstage like his idol, James Brown. There never seemed to be any doubt in Michael Christian's mind about that. For now, he just wanted to see "The Birds" while he pretended to be James Brown in the Hospital.

Pretending to be James Brown in the Hospital was not without its hazards for Michael Christian; he had to remember to keep his head lifted from his pillow so as not to *bedhead* his budding Afro. Once, when he was practicing his singing, the nurses rushed to his bed asking him where it hurt.

"I'm warming up 'I Feel Good,' stupid bitches," said Michael Christian. Then his bed was jerked from the wall and wheeled with great speed, pushed and pulled along by hissing nurses, jarring other bedsteads, Michael Christian's wrists hanging over the safety bedrails like jailhouse-window hands; he was on his way to spend a couple of solitary hours out in the long, dark, and empty hall, him rolling his eyes at me as he sped past, saying, "Aw, man, now I feel BAD!"

Bed wheeling into the hall was one of the few alternatives to corporal punishment the nurses had, most of them being reluctant to spank a child in traction for spitting an orange pip at his neighbor, or to beat a completely burned child for cursing. Bed wheeling into the hall was especially effective at Christmastime, when it carried the possibility of missing Christmas programs. A veteran of several Christmases in the Hospital and well acquainted with the grim Christmas programs, Michael Christian scoffed at the treasures handed out by the church and state charities—the aging fruit, the surplus ballpoint pens, the occasional batches of recycled toys that didn't work, the games and puzzles with missing pieces. Michael Christian's Christmas Wish was as specific as mine. I wanted a miniature train set with batteries so I could lay out the track to run around my bed over the covers. Not the big Lionel size or the HO size. I wanted the set you could see in magazines, where they show you the actual size of the railroad engine as being no larger than a walnut.

"You never get that, man," Michael Christian said, and he was right.

James Brown in the Hospital's Christmas Wish was for "The Birds" for Christmas. And, as Michael Christian's friend, I became an accomplice in his desire. In that way, "birds" became a code, the way words can among boys.

"Gimme some BIRDS!" Michael Christian would squawk

when the society ladies on their annual Christmas visit asked us what we wanted.

"How about a nice hairbrush?" a society lady said, laying one for white people at the foot of Michael Christian's bed.

"I want a pick," Michael Christian told her.

"A pick? A shovel and a pick? To dig with?" asked the society lady.

"I think he wants a comb for his hair," I said. "For his Afro."

"That's right: a pick," said Michael Christian. "Tell this stupid white bitch something. *Squawk, squawk,"* he said, flapping his elbows like wings, as the nurses wheeled him out into the hall. "Gimme some BIRDS!" he shouted, and when they asked me, I said to give me some birds, too.

Michael Christian's boldness over the Christmas programs increased when Ben, the night porter, broke the television. Looking back, it may not be fair to say that Ben, the night porter, actually broke the television, but one evening it was soundlessly playing some kiddie Christmas show and Ben was standing near it mopping up a spilt urinal can when the screen and the hope of Michael Christian's getting his Christmas Wish blackened simultaneously. Apologetic at first, knowing what even a soundless television meant to children who had rarely seen any television at all, Ben then offered to "burn up your butt, Michael Christian, legs braces and all" when Michael Christian hissed "stupid nigger" at Ben, beneath the night nurse's hearing. It was a somber Lights Out.

The next night, a priest and some students from the seminary came by. Practice Preachers, Michael Christian said. While one of the students read the Christmas story from the Bible, Michael Christian pretended to peck his own eyes out with pinched fingers. When the story was finished, Michael Christian said, "Now, you say the sheepherding guys was so afraid, right?"

"*Sore* afraid," said the Practice Preacher. "The shepherds had never seen angels before, and they were *sore* afraid."

"Naw," said Michael Christian. "I'll tell you what—they saw these big white things flapping down and they was big *birds*, man. I know *birds*, man, I know when you got bird *problems,* man."

"They were *angels,*" said the young seminary student.

"Naw," said Michael Christian. "They was big white birds, and the sheepherding guys were *so* afraid the big white birds was swooping down and getting all up in they *hair* and stuff! *Squawk, squawk!*" he said, flapping around in his bed.

"Squawk, squawk!" I answered, and two of the Practice Preachers assisted the nurses in wheeling Michael Christian into the hall and me into the linen cupboard.

One night in the week before Christmas, a man named Sammy came to visit. He had been a patient as a child, and his botched cleft-palate and harelip repairs were barely concealed by a weird line of blond mustache. Sammy owned a hauling company now, and he showed up blistering drunk, wearing a ratty Santa suit, and began handing out black-strapped Timex Junior wristwatches. I still have mine, somewhere.

One by one we told Sammy what we wanted for Christmas, even though we were not sure, because of his speech defect, that that was what he was asking. Me, the walnut train; Michael Christian, "The Birds." We answered without enthusiasm, without hope: it was all by rote. By the end of the visit, Sammy was a blubbering sentimental mess, reeking of alcohol and promises. Ben, the night porter, put him out.

It was Christmas Eve week. The boy who kept running away finally ran away for good. Before he left, he snatched the dime from the channel selector on our broken TV. We all saw him do it and we didn't care. We didn't even yell out to the night nurse, so he could get a better head start than usual.

It was Christmas Eve week, and Michael Christian lay listless in his bed. We watched the Big Boy ward empty. Somebody even came for one of the moaners, and the guy out on the sun porch was sent upstairs for a final visit to the Young Doctors so they could finish taking him apart.

On the night before Christmas Eve, Michael Christian and I heard street shoes clicking down the long corridor that led to where we lay. It was after lights out. We watched and waited and waited. It was just Sammy the Santa, except this time he was wearing a pale-blue leisure suit, his hair was oiled back, and his hands, holding a redwrapped box, were clean.

What we did not want for Christmas were wristwatches. What we did not want for Christmas were bars of soap. We did not want any more candy canes, bookmarks, ballpoint pens, or somebody else's last year's broken toy. For Christmas we did not want plastic crosses, dot books, or fruit baskets. No more handshakes, head pats, or storybook times. It was the night before Christmas Eve, and Michael Christian had not mentioned "The Birds" in days, and I had given up on the walnut train. We did not want any more Christmas Wishes.

Sammy spoke with the night nurse, we heard him plead that it was Christmas, and she said all right, and by her flashlight she brought him to us. In the yellow spread of her weak batteries, we watched Michael Christian unwrap a portable television.

There was nothing to be done except plug the television into the wall. It was Christmas, Sammy coaxed the reluctant night nurse. They put the little TV on a chair and we watched the end of an Andy Williams Christmas Special. We watched the eleven-o'clock news. Then the movie began: "The Birds." It was Christmas, Sammy convinced the night nurse.

The night nurse wheeled her chair away from the chart table and rolled it to the television set. The volume was low, so as not to disturb the damaged babies at the Little Boy end of the ward—babies largely uncollected until after the holidays, if at all. Sammy sat on an empty bed. He patted it. Michael Christian and I watched "The Birds."

During the commercials, the night nurse checked the hall for the supervisor. Sammy helped her turn any infant that cried out.

The night nurse let Sammy have some extra pillows. Michael Christian spoke to me only once during a commercial when we were alone, he said, "Those birds messing them people *up*."

When the movie was over, it was the first hours of Christmas Eve. The night nurse woke Sammy and let him out through the sun porch. She told us to go to sleep, and rolled her chair back to her chart table. In the emptiness you could hear the metal charts click and scratch, her folds of white starch rustle. Through a hole in the pony blanket I had pulled over my head I could see Michael Christian's bed. His precious Afro head was buried deep beneath his pillow.

At the dark end of the ward a baby cried in its sleep and then was still.

It was Christmas Eve, and we were sore afraid.

Occasion for Repentance

by Kay Sloan

A yellow half-moon crept over the mossy oak tree in Hinton Renfro's yard on Flamingo Road in Biloxi, Mississippi. The light made Hinton uneasy, especially with the approaching sound of Christmas carolers down the street. He was naked, watering his oleander hedge with the garden hose wrapped several times around his paunch. In one hand, he clutched the third beer of the night's six pack, while the thumb of the other hand forced the water into an arc that shot at the center of each plant.

Right down to the roots, he thought triumphantly. It was one of those rare moments when he felt more angry than sad that his wife, Lucinda, had left him. One desperate night soon after Lucinda left at Thanksgiving, he rearranged their clothes in the closet, smelling her sweaters, putting one pair of his pants between each of her skirts and one of his shirts between each of her blouses, then pressing the hangers together. It was a poor substitute for sex, and now he rarely opened the closet, preferring instead to live in his old sweatpants. On the top shelf, nestled in a baseball cap, lay a small box wrapped in reindeer gift paper. He was considering giving the silver and turquoise necklace he'd bought for Lucinda in Ocean Springs to his mother. Some holiday. And Christmas carols, all the jolly good cheer, what a nightmare.

There was no escape. Across the street, a door opened and Bing Crosby's voice swelled into the night, dreams of a white Christmas. From his neighbor's front steps came the sounds of a muffled conversation. Someone was leaving. The houses all looked alike here, each with driveways of crushed oyster shells. Even the Christmas decorations were similar, multicolored lights flashing on shrubs, wreaths with artificial pinecones suspended on front doors. The only thing that distinguished his own house was the congregation of pink ceramic flamingos Lucinda had planted in the front yard on wire stakes, to give a little humorous credibility to the street's name when they moved in the summer before. He'd put Santa's elves on the backs of two flamingos, a half-hearted concession to the season. Without Lucinda, he wasn't capable of decorating a tree, too many memories attached to the ornaments they had accumulated in eight years of marriage.

"Bye, Evan," came a female voice from across the street. "You have yourself a merry little Christmas, hear? I'll see you New Year's Eve. We'll just blow this ole year away in high style. Whoo-ee!"

Through the hedge, Hinton spied a woman in a white rabbit-fur jacket and tight jeans that ended in spike heels. She was standing beside the flickering lights on a cedar tree at his neighbor's open front door. Red, blue, green, and silver—the lights sparkled in quick succession, then flashed simultaneously, as if the tree might be wired in Morse code.

Hinton saw her glance toward his own house, and on an impulse, he crouched, then realized there was nothing but the scrawny hedge to hide behind. What would they think of a naked man hiding on his own front lawn? He stood upright again. In a lower voice, she was asking, "How's that weirdo across the street? Still watering his flowers in the dead of winter?" She let out a hoot. "Maybe he's giving those tacky flamingos a drink."

"The elves look a tad tight, don't they?" It was his neighbor's voice.

Who cared? thought Hinton. He'd been called a weirdo before, though for better reasons than watering his hedge off-season. And he was sure someone had called him worse things. The woman obviously had no sense of the ironic. Lucinda had been forced to explain the concept to her own mother, who worried that people would think they were trash. "Trailer-park taste," his mother-in-law had said, when the first flamingo appeared.

"You might as well be living across from a trailer park." His neighbor's guest giggled as if she'd read Hinton's mind.

Hinton scowled at her rabbit fur. Idiot, he thought. She must be broiling under that thing. His neighbor snickered, then murmured something under his breath. More loudly, he laughed, "Maybe the guy's an alien."

"Well, he's downright spooky, if you ask me," she replied, walking toward her car at the curb.

"The guy's got some smarts," said his neighbor, and Hinton felt a surge of loyalty to him, despite the "Honk If You Believe in Santa" bumper sticker on his shiny red BMW. "The newspaper said he made a movie about the ozone, almost won some kind of award out in California. They ran a picture of him. Didn't look so crazy."

"Excuse me? A guy puts elves on flamingos isn't a little nuts? Walks around naked in the dead of winter? C'mon."

God, she'd seen him.

"You oughtta call the cops." The click of her high heels echoed against concrete. She was walking toward her car at the curb.

"Bah-bah, dahlin," came his neighbor's voice.

The sound reminded Hinton more of a sheep than a man. My god, he thought, if the accent were phony it wouldn't seem quite so bizarre. But that was just it. They were real, those sounds that came from human throats. These Gulf Coast types were a strange breed, spacey and offbeat, as if the heat of too many summers had swelled their brains, and they could communicate only in monosyllables or in subtle shifts of their eyes. They seemed to have a collective language that had never been documented by any anthropologist.

Hinton aimed the hose at one of the bare oleander limbs and sent water droplets scattering in all directions like silver buckshot. The moon leered from the safety of its perch in the oak tree. Had the hose been powerful enough, he would have shot it down, too. It was a good night to release some frustration.

The Sun Belt propaganda, he had learned fast, was a lie. There was no easy living here. In a downwind, he could smell the stench of decaying crustaceans that the neighbor kids pulled from conch shells just for fun, leaving the carcasses to rot on the driveway. And so what if you could go naked in the middle of December? He longed for the Pacific Ocean, even the gray coastal fog. Sometimes he even grew nostalgic for the smug film students he had taught at Central Aquarius College, all hoping to be the next generation's superstars, a new Spielberg, or, for the more artsy ones, a new Tarentino. But when the college administrators had slashed the budget, they cut out his position, sending him scuttling for a job. When he was a graduate student at Berkeley, he'd had a radio show on KZEN, calling himself Brother Jupiter, and the manager had made him an offer to come back just as Lucinda talked him into moving to Biloxi instead. They could spend an old-fashioned Christmas with her family up in the Delta, she'd said. Now her folks had bought tickets to Cancun for the holidays.

Nothing lasted, nothing could be counted on anymore. The older he got, the more things shifted and slid from his grasp. Even the first experimental films he had made, geometric bursts of color like celluloid fireworks, had split and faded. His last film in Berkeley had been a documentary on how the ozone erosion was altering the climate. It won an Academy Award nomination, but no cigar. He'd hoped that some new funding might pay off the price of the designer dress Lucinda wore to the festivities, but so far there'd been no producers knocking at his door.

The water spray sputtered in Hinton's hand, and he jumped, startled at the jerking. Then he reached down to untwist a knot that had tangled the hose. The spray shot out with a new vengeance. He fired an elf off a flamingo, knocked it three feet into the muddy sand, then aimed the nozzle at the next plant's roots.

Even his home was temporary, he thought. He had wanted to stay in Berkeley, but Lucinda persuaded him to settle in this outpost of civilization on the Gulf Coast. She made jewelry to sell on eBay, and she was tired of the inspiration she got in California. Artists needed change, she said, and the Gulf Coast islands had all kinds of shells she could use in necklaces and earrings, great for Christmas sales. She'd grown up, after all, in Biloxi, floundering and crabbing in the Gulf waters at night, long after other kids her age were tucked in bed. He used to tease her: she was a rebel, not a Southern belle but a re-belle.

News of spaceship sightings from south Mississippi had only enticed her more. From Pascagoula, CNN's Anderson Cooper, undecided whether to look worried or amused, covered the story of Rafe Jenkins and his family, held hostage for two full days onboard an alien craft. Later, *First Edition* interviewed one of Lucinda's old schoolteachers, when she'd found a circle burned in her tomato garden. When *Time* devoted its cover to the phenomenal hysteria gripping the region, Lucinda couldn't wait to move back. A special report on the local TV station, WLOX, called Mississippi the new "chosen land."

Lucinda was convinced that living in Biloxi would inspire a new line of futuristic earrings and pendants. Everyone, it seemed, had spotted weird creatures or unexplainable lights or heard eerie, otherworldly noises on deserted back roads. Lately, Hinton had noticed that everything looked a little strange to him, too. Hell, even the enormous kitchen roaches looked like invaders from space.

In the distance, a siren wailed out into the night, drowning out the carolers' version of "We Wish You a Merry Christmas." Had his neighbor called the cops? Hinton frowned, concentrating on the direction of the wail before making a dash indoors. It dwindled in the direction of Biloxi General. An ambulance, a street-bound shooting star.

At Factrax, where Hinton had landed a job making industrial training films of happy workers on assembly lines, almost everyone had seen mysterious lights hovering out over the Gulf or zipping through the sky, fast as a shooting star. What a terrific film that would make! Though Lucinda complained about never seeing him, he'd begun to spend more and more time at the factory, interviewing the workers, shooting footage while they told him their stories. Lucinda had been upset when he'd stayed out all night with Kristle Kramer, the union leader, and it had been impossible to persuade her that he'd been shooting footage all night. All he'd gotten was a lot of grief from Lucinda. It hadn't helped that Kristle had once been a beauty queen, "Miss Congenial" in the Miss Mississippi pageant ten years before.

"So that's why you're at the factory all the time! Just to be with a left-over beauty queen. I can't believe you'd fall for a loser like that!" Lucinda hissed when he'd come home at 5 a.m. He tried to explain where he'd been, but she kept interrupting, and finally broke into tears.

"Do you know what those people thought of me when I was growing up here? I was just a weirdo to them. Do you think I was ever in a talent show? And here you are, hanging out with a beauty queen! One of *them!*"

He'd never seen her so upset. This wasn't the Lucinda he knew. The woman he married in Berkeley was charming and confident. It was as if he'd kicked over a stone in her psyche and found strange creatures crawling beneath.

He took her in his arms and squeezed her. "Don't be jealous. Sure, she's really gorgeous and all that, but you're the one I love."

"You idiot," she said and shoved him away.

"What?"

"You've never once said I'm gorgeous. Not once. Ever."

"I didn't think you cared about looks." He tried to laugh but her eyes could have fried him. "Wouldn't have married *me* if you did." But nothing he could say could make up the difference. She packed up three suitcases and went to Miami Beach to spend Thanksgiving with a cousin named Luther who drew portraits of tourists on the boardwalks. Talk about weird. But Lucinda hadn't come back. Not even with Christmas only a week away.

The oleanders sagged under the jets of water he had fired at them. He polished off his Budweiser, turned off the hose, and unwound himself from its pleasantly cool tangles. Not a bad way to pass these lonely, balmy nights. A breeze teased Lucinda's porch wind chimes, strings of shells that she'd found on Ship Island. It sounded like she'd left some of her laughter behind.

Hinton closed the kitchen door against the tinkle and turned on the television in the den. *A Christmas Miracle,* with Hillary Duff as a missionary's daughter in China, was starting up. He turned off the sound and hit the red button flashing on his answering machine before heading toward the refrigerator. His mother's voice blared into the room. "It's your mother. What, you don't remember to call your mother at Christmas? I've forgotten what you look like, it's been so long. We never hear from you and Lucinda anymore." There was a pause, then came the scolding voice he remembered as a kid. "If you're screening this, Hinton, pick up the telephone. I'm checking into flights to come out for Christmas." She waited a minute, then came the click of a hang up.

He froze, one hand on a bag of bagels. No, she wouldn't leave California at Christmas, he thought, and ran a hand through his hair. Not with the new boyfriend in San Diego. How did she always know when he and Lucinda were having "marital problems," as she called it? He shuddered at the words.

He reached into the refrigerator in search of the last beer. Odd, he thought. Had he already drunk the damn thing? He searched the refrigerator shelves, moving aside the empty butter dish and the moldy remains of a pizza, rearranging the dozen or so pints of lemon yogurt, lifting his sack of onion bagels. Not a clue. The refrigerator light flickered, as if to shrug its own confusion, and then went out.

It must be, as Lucinda would say, a sign. She would probably advise him to get out the *Book of Changes* and throw the I Ching coins for some insight. She had thrown her three bronze Oriental coins to determine whether she should leave for Thanksgiving. The hexagram, as always, was ambiguous, and they'd quarreled over how to interpret it, with Lucinda insisting that the "new bridge" it mentioned was part of her path away from him, not a reconciliation between the two of them. He saddened at the memory and closed the refrigerator.

"Advantage will come from being firm and correct," he had taunted her with a quote from the book. "Occasion for repentance will disappear." He remembered the exact words and remembered just as well how he had sneered it at Lucinda. He had ripped out the page on the Ko hexagram from her cherished *Book of Changes,* wadded it into a missile, and fired it at her.

White-faced and shaking, Lucinda had calmly gathered up her coins and tattered book and strode toward the door. Before getting even halfway there, she suddenly grabbed their hanging fern from its hook, turned, and hurled it in the direction of his receding hairline. It missed.

They had woken the next morning in each other's arms and begun the day by picking crushed fern leaves out of the shag carpet. They both cried over the broken plant, a wedding gift from Lucinda's young cousin who lived on some mountain in Santa Cruz, California. Hinton had never met her, but all of Lucinda's cousins were flaky. She had decorated the plant with a set of tiny playing cards, each dangling from a green frond.

"Hope you two always play with a full deck!" she'd scrawled on a card that read, "Congratulations to the Newly Weds!"

Giving up the plant for dead, Lucinda had taken the macramé holder her cousin had knotted, but somehow Hinton coaxed the plant into sending up new shoots. It would recover. Bits of withered brown fronds clogged the Hoover bag when he vacuumed. He found one of her bronze coins there among the dust in the bag, started to send it to her cousin's address as a gesture of goodwill, and changed his mind. If she just hadn't thrown the I Ching.

He'd be damned if he was going to dig up three pennies to tell him where his last beer was. He pulled on cutoffs and an Oakland Warriors sweatshirt to dash up to the corner Pack-A-Sack-And-Tote-Sum for another six pack. The key clicked into his Volvo's ignition and clicked again when he turned it. His stomach sank. Damn. It clicked again. And again. He slumped in the worn seat. The starter, he sighed, slamming the door shut. Nothing major, he assured himself, as he slipped his bare feet into running shoes to stroll the five blocks up to the store. Nice night for a walk, anyway.

Lucinda always told him he didn't exercise enough; his new Right Balance shoes were a gift from her to get him to jog. Jog! She would bound all aglow and self-righteously sweating from her workouts at the Gulfport Y and fret over the condition of his heart. Was she happy now that she'd broken it? He rolled his eyes at his own thought. A few beers, and he was waxing maudlin.

He eased her from his mind as he walked, thinking of his film on the rash of alien sightings at Factrax. He wanted to experiment with video, odd soundtracks, and he hoped, a subversive comment on assembly lines and the kind of fantasies workers had. Or was that too dramatic, too exaggerated? Lucinda always said he pushed things too far, but forget Lucinda. It could work, especially with a dynamite soundtrack to make it surreal. Some Lou Reed, say, or Jonathan Richman, along with the eerie whirring that always accompanied the conveyer belts at Factrax.

Since he hadn't bothered to pull on socks, his left jogging shoe was rubbing a blister on his heel. He barely noticed the pain, too busy with plans for his film to pay attention to that minor irritation, or to the little suburban houses that usually made him shudder when he passed, with their identical two-car garages and oleander hedges.

This could be an important film, he told himself. Maybe he could make an entire series of UFO documentaries down here. *That,* at least, would interest Lucinda. He smiled at the possibilities; he could almost hear the whirring.

The full moon had risen further, as if smiling down on him. It gleamed a golden approval. But something was odd about it.

He stopped. My god, he thought. He turned on his blistered heel and looked in the sky behind him. The moon still hung, like a half-shut eye winking at him from the east. What the hell *was* this thing? An airplane, he told himself. It was moving toward him, that's why it appeared stationary while it got bigger. His heart thumped as the vision of the terrified family that Anderson Cooper had interviewed on television flashed through his mind. Rafe Jenkins, father of five, had described a huge orb of luminous white light that descended and blocked his station wagon in a lonely fishing camp. Two days, it had been, according to the calendar, and none of the Jenkins could even remember what had happened. Rafe Jenkins beamed like he'd drunk a whole flask of moonshine. "Looked just like heaven," he'd said. "Like those pictures in the Bible." It hadn't helped their national credibility.

But, holy cow, this thing was moving! Hinton braced his back against a neighbor's chain-link fence and stared. A hot-air balloon? The wind couldn't possibly move it that fast, and there was barely a breeze. And a helluva shooting star, if that's what it was.

Maybe his mother had arranged her Christmas flight with Martians. He tried to make a chuckle come out of his throat, but the noise sounded strangled. Behind the fence, a German shepherd whimpered. He turned to shush the dog, and when he turned back the light was coming still closer, noiselessly. Were those windows?

He felt giddy, mesmerized by the glowing silence. Something was falling from the sky, descending like a light hail, striking the sidewalk around him. A sharp pain jolted his forehead, and he dived to the concrete, covering his head with his arms, shielding from his sight those two-car garages and neatly trimmed oleander hedges.

Katie Couric smiled at Hinton.

He adjusted his tie, red for television, ran his hand through his hair, and flicked a cigarette ash from the sleeve of his coat. A square white bandage covered his forehead over his left eye.

"Just talk to me." She put a comforting hand on his sleeve. "It's as if we're simply having a conversation."

Sure, he thought, some conversation. One that jeopardized his job, his friends, his marriage, his entire future. His mother had cried over the telephone from Fresno. Factrax had threatened him with dismissal for the two days when he failed to report to work unless he went to a psychiatrist for hypnosis. And the Air Force! They wanted to "debrief" him, for chrissake. Now both Katie Couric and Gerry Rivers, who billed himself as "the talk show host who talks to anybody," wanted to interview him for their shows. From Hollywood, a producer at Torpedo Films had called Hinton about the rights to his story, giving him the option of writing the first version of the script himself.

And Lucinda? She was making him the hero of her new story. She wanted the tapes from the psychiatric session he had spent under hypnosis. No way, Hinton thought. His psychiatrist, of course, wouldn't divulge their contents. Whatever he had to say, Hinton Renfro would say it to the country, and to hell with the consequences.

But how could he explain the euphoria that Rafe Jenkins had described before he went blank? The best story Hinton could imagine was making love with Lucinda one glorious night in the Napa countryside before they married. Most people probably wouldn't understand that. Katie Couric might not. But Lucinda would know. And without Lucinda, life would never be the same for him, whether he told his story or not. So why not go for broke? Besides, the public had a right to hear the story from someone who could tell it better than Rafe Jenkins.

Hinton smiled at Katie.

"You were wonderful." Lucinda hugged him at the New Orleans airport when he arrived from New York. She'd left a message at his hotel saying she'd be waiting for his flight if he would call her at home and let her know when it landed. Home! he had thought. Exactly where is she living now? When he'd dialed the number on Flamingo Road, she had answered and immediately begun peppering him with questions not about Kristle Kramer's congeniality but about the script for *Two Days*.

Now, he sucked in his beer belly when she pressed herself against him, flattening himself to feel the curves of her body more fully. He closed his eyes, enjoying the strangely familiar sensation, remembering.

"Was it really like that night in the wine country?" Lucinda pulled away and beamed up at him. "I can't believe you said that on the air. Mama called to make sure it happened *after* we married—I told her sure, you were just nervous and got confused. But you didn't even look nervous. Did those creatures really look like blue lights? And their eyes—how weird."

"They weren't exactly weird. It was like they could see right through me. The way you used to look at me, sometimes." He grinned down at her, but she wasn't listening.

"Why do you think they chose you? What was Katie Couric like? Did she look old? And the Gerry Rivers Show next week! I can't wait to hear what that guy's like!"

"I follow a bunch of five year olds who're still breastfeeding. Some kind of ten-step program for addicts . . ."

But she didn't hear. "Why did your watch stop for two days? Tell me about the movie you're writing about it. You need a better title . . ."

He could hardly hear her words, much less find the space between them to answer. The airport buzzed with the noises of flights being announced, with porters rolling baggage carts loaded with Christmas presents, and with the sounds of human beings greeting and parting in a vast orderly confusion. The sound came to him like the babble of animals, the tongue of a species that had become foreign, the female sounds a pocket of higher octaves, the males a guttural thud, like an abstract musical composition in which the notes intertwined through the flowing air. He could've been a composer, he thought.

He stepped onto a moving walkway with Lucinda, and together they strode forward rapidly, their steps accelerated by the speed already beneath them. He felt as though his ankles had suddenly grown tiny wings. Lucinda's arm wove familiarly through his, and he could feel the warm pressure of her breast against his arm as they moved toward the baggage claim.

The morning sun stretched long shadows across the bed, slanting its way through matchstick blinds. Lucinda lay curled beside him, stroking the silver and turquoise necklace at her throat. He had handed her the box in its reindeer paper when they'd gotten in the night before, with a note, "You're the most gorgeous woman I know." She cried so hard he had to help her open the present, and then she'd cried more when she saw the necklace.

She had brought him one of her cousin Luther's recent drawings, tucked into a cylindrical cardboard tube with only a gift tag stuck on for decoration. He pulled it out, preparing to be polite, but it was stunning. Luther had overlaid an ancient Greek map of the cosmos and a medieval map of the flat world, making constellations appear in oddly shaped, sepia-colored oceans. A Celtic calendar formed the frame.

"It seemed perfect for you," she said, looking from the drawing to Hinton. "I had to beg Luther to sell it."

"This is amazing," he said, wondering if Luther could possibly have done it himself. A pang of guilt nudged at him, and he laid the drawing gently on the dining table. It was Christmas, after all. He could believe Luther was a real artist at least for a day or two. That would be some miracle. "Let's pick up a tree tomorrow. There's bound to be some scraggly little fir left in need of a good home," he said and folded her into his arms.

Now, even after only a few hours of sleep, she was wired. She was restraining herself from waking Hinton by imagining him on board the spaceship, surrounded by the strange blue creatures he'd described to Katie Couric.

"Lordy, Hinton," she sighed when he began to open his eyes. "What if they had taken you?"

Maybe they had, he thought, twitching his toes happily beneath the covers. Maybe they had. Maybe calendar printers and map makers had invented time and space. The map and calendar makers were just like Barnum & Bailey marketing the circus—they could create whole worlds at the same time they made their living.

And we all bought it like dutiful consumers, Hinton thought. Like the way Christmas had been bought, with SUVs jamming the mall parking lots and frantic kids begging for iPods and cell phones. The only miracle left was that parents paid off their credit cards before the next Christmas.

But maybe Rafe Jenkins was a little miracle, one man beaming into television cameras to claim that he'd seen heaven.

Hinton still hadn't reset his watch. He wore it on his wrist, its hands stuck at the time he had fallen to the sidewalk, like a badge or a war medal. 9:26 p.m. He would let other people, those oblivious dancers on the walls of Plato's cave, keep watch repairers in business, buying time with their wrinkles, their deadlines.

"Well, I'm here now, babe. And so are you. Best Christmas present I could have."

He rolled over to avoid the ray of sunlight that was edging toward his right eye and reached for Lucinda.

The Cold Giraffe

by Olympia Vernon

She wanted to eat snow.

Of course, she wanted to take it all down—into her stomach—and swallow.

Her finger rose up toward the window where a child had written, *You ain't no good.*

The phosphoric tail of a dragon confined the white hairs of her head; she appeared in the eye of a bird to resemble an oar. Of course, her mother had pushed her out of the womb and shaped her with her hips, so that she appeared linear, anemic, flattened out.

It was the laughter of children she heard; they were running about, each darting in and out of snow, each collapsing under a white cloud, clinging invisibly to the white, as if injected by the momentary absence of the sun.

Yes, she stood there as a great oar. She had come from a thin and fragile vein here in Ellis County, Mississippi—wood carvers and blacksmiths; she had adjusted herself to the first, the wood carvers, and now, now, she thought of it; she thought of the giraffe.

Yes, yes, yes, it had been the first; the first stroke, the very first of all pressures. Her thumb bled; she had worn a blouse—bone white it was—and it was dotted with crimson, as if an ox had been slain.

Tuck coughed.

How many years now had she clung to him? To his and her matrimony where it seemed two people, this Christmas, had succumbed to some sort of silence in this house?

Perhaps, it was that awful piano of, of, of the Darner wife that woke him. Of course, she was sitting near the window of her house across the road—this was the house the children had begun to inject with the injection forced upon them; they panted loudly upon the tracks of snow, falling and pointing with their index fingers through the lens of the injection, the syringe. They neared the steps of the Darner wife, yelled, one to another, something of the wife and her stiffness; they imitated her posture, mocked her, poked and poked and poked her.

But the Darner wife played on; yes, yes, she saw Ferst from the window with that dreadful pin in her hair, that awful pin of the dead. Hadn't her mother died with that pin in her hair? she thought. What was it? The tail of a dragon?

A young girl— with her round face and body—abandoned the Darner wife's porch and joined the others who were now marching up the road, laughing and holding their bellies, as the Darner wife had come out of her house now and stood near the tracing of the young girl with her fist in the air: *Let go,* it read.

A glacier eased through her face and shattered.

She closed the door of her house and played ever more vigorously, as if what had been written, said, injected about and into her was now . . . fascinating.

Tuck coughed.

It *was* the piano, that, that awful key. What key was it? he thought.

It played on and on and on and on, and it seemed to have played with the coughing up of blood, the spilling of things. It played on and on with the dotted oxygen, the weakening of the bones, the anemic invasion, and she wouldn't stop playing it—the Darner wife—not even this Christmas would she stop playing it, and she had told them that.

Now, Ferst stood in the mouth of the door.

The phosphoric tail of the dragon-tailed pin bled into the room with its light; it bled and shaped its bleeding throughout. She was linear, anemic, flattened out.

An umbilical cord had been clipped somewhere in the Universe.

A match had been struck in this room.

And she knew it.

Tuck's foot jutted out from the Eye of the covers; the bed, centered and clasped to the womb of this, this episode, caused his face to turn away from the . . . only Ferst did he know was in this world and only did he think of other things, memories, artifacts when her shadow was shaped in them.

He summoned her.

But Ferst did not go.

How long now had the Good Doctor come to tell her the news? she thought.

She could neither remember nor forget.

Ferst, the Good Doctor whispered, he's done low.

The bones of her anatomy had failed to keep her. She had simply fainted.

Ferst . . . Ferst, whispered the Good Doctor, he's done low. He's done low and you've, you've gotta tote 'm.

Indeed, Tuck had summoned her.

And he had summoned her like this when he'd swallowed blood—he was of that kind and age then—her blouse was dotted with crimson, and a piano had been playing. The snow, the snow . . . he could remember its having snowed only three times, and this, this was the third . . . and a piano had been playing, and a layer of snow had coated the window, and they, he and Ferst, had stood in it, together, with her blood in his mouth.

There were photographs in this room—one of him and her; one of her on the steps of the courthouse with her hands clasped, her face at her shoe; one of her squatting near the Mississippi; and that one, that one photo of her in the camera's eye, the red kite of the Darner husband dotting the lens.

Ferst reeked of the key.

She gathered her gown at its hem—bone white it was—and lifted it over her head, and thus, the white hairs of her head had begun to leak out of the dragon-tailed pin.

Tuck stretched his arm out beside him, hid his face in his shoulder. He wanted to eat snow; his stomach was burning; his pale throat and lungs burned with the phosphoric temperature and glow of a memory, a germ, a key. Oh, how it played on and on and gathered around and about him with its invisible injection, its gradual weave, its mockery.

I hear it, he whispered.

The dragon-tailed pin had come loose from Ferst's hair; the white leaked out of it and onto the floor. She had positioned herself on the bridge of his arm; it was wet under the covers—the sweat and odor of a burning—and he let her, he let her turn away from him like that and writhe in her gown with the white leaking out of her hair. She turned and spun with the resistance of the key; he could not have imagined this scene without her in it. Only had he hoped, wished that she'd been . . . in it . . . that perhaps, he'd become entangled in the line, that he'd kiss her and the blood of the cold giraffe would . . . there was the sound of children; they were returning on the open road, and he could hear them trudging through the slush and rib of the sun's absence.

His hand had begun to quiver.

He wanted to eat snow.

There was only one burning, one stroke, one first of all pressures, one . . . this was when he reached for it—it was there beneath the covers—he clung to it, brought it up to his face with the simultaneous injection of the blood, the key.

The cold giraffe was trapped in her eye.

And the children trudged through the slush and rib of the sun's absence, and the piano played on and on with its dotted oxygen, its posture, its mockery, and thus, she turned to face him, whispered, I see it, but the rigor mortis of the dragon-tailed pin had crept into his eyelid . . . let him go.

HOME
SWE
HOM

Novena

by Suzanne Hudson

The upstairs room where Leila's daughter slept was peaceful by design. Baseboards of powder blue blended imperceptibly into baby blue, then deepening blue walls rising and meshing into a ceiling the blue-black of midnight blue, a scattering of clouds and faint stars all around and above, glowing reassurance in the dimness. The Virgin Mary kept watch from a painting above the bed, and an elaborately carved crucifix guarded her daughter's dreams. Trish was curled kitten-like beneath her great-grandmother's satin comforter while nonstop Christmas music over the intercom muted potential Santa sounds below. The coast was clear.

Amber-honeyed strains of Johnny Mathis washed over Leila as she descended the stairs to the living room, longing for a dance with Joe, missing her co-conspirator in the Santa game, but business had taken her husband out of town until tomorrow, Christmas morning. Leila hugged her shoulders, dismissing the resentment, knowing that this Christmas, though a struggle certainly, was worlds better than last year's. Last year the earth had stopped turning, slinging planets, stars, the sun, and her heart crazily out of orbit, into a yawning black hole.

The tree glimmered iridescent, hushed, tinseled pinwheelings of light, sliced and thrown through Scotch pine scents. Flashes of red, gold, and green, tissue-papered, wore dotted Swiss bows of blue and yellow, all a crescendo mounting for the next light, the first light.

Elsewhere in the house—the dining room, the den, her own bedroom, and, until last year, the music room that now housed her mother's piano alongside her own—were color-coordinated Christmas trees, elegant, elegiac, sterile with fixed ribbons, orchids with the stomach-turning scent that flowers had become, and fretful angels, talismans set upon triangles, all worthy of being window dressing at the floral shops she owned.

But this tree—a hodge-podge of passed-down baubles, ticky-tacky handmade ornaments from ancient school days (her brothers' cotton-balled Santas, her own disintegrating tinfoil-covered cardboard stars—decorations she had taken from her mother's stored boxes only eight days ago, on the anniversary of her death)—this tree was the one that held hostage her Yuletide spirit. Thin satin ribbons dangled ancestral visages, framed among the spiky branches that were emerald in the light, forest green behind it. And among the pictures of her seven-year-old daughter, juxtaposed with long-deceased greats and great-greats, were pictures of Leila's twin brothers: Coleman, lost to Vietnam when Leila was only eight, and

Curtis lost just six years ago to a decayed liver awash in gin, guilt, and a bitter longing for the brother who completed him. There, too, were her parents, both buried after the previous year's shopping trip ended in a flaming collision with an eighteen-wheeler, arching the car across the blacktop like a shooting star in her nightmares. And finally, thankfully, Leila's eyes settled upon a flapperesque image of MamaLee, her grandmother, the only forebear still living, filling the blank, barren fields between Leila and her own mortality.

Leila had visited MamaLee at the Bayside Nursing Home just five days ago, the one-hundred mile drive to Mobile made in a frustrated rush of emotion after she hung her mother's ornaments on the tree, covering its branches, really, so determined was she to use everything her mother had fastidiously packed away. The eyes of the elderly in the wheelchair-lined hallways unnerved her, made her feel embarrassed at some kind of shared secret, the naked vulnerability that came with Death's quickening step.

The whispered scents of alcohol, pine cleaner, Vicks' VaporRub, and soiled sheets found Leila; during her brief visit they would become as oppressive as the scents of roses and gardenias at her parents' funeral and at her shops, where the heady floral odor she once loved would now sting her eyes, nauseating, until she had to leave for air.

The old woman's bed was the same spool bed (fitted now with an electric hospital mattress) that she had been birthed in, given birth to her only child in, and seemed poised and rehearsing to die in. A gaggle of nurses, led by a dictator of a head nurse who bore several clichéd, derogatory nicknames, had festooned the bed with an artificial garland and placed a crown of foil stars upon the purplish pouf of a bun MamaLee wore. The red stars clashed hideously with the loosened cotton-candy strands of hair, and Leila took the crown off to smooth her grandmother's hair back into place, make it right. MamaLee was beautiful, Leila thought, with the periwinkle eyes of Leila's mother and delicately wrinkled baby-smooth skin, powdered down and lightly rouged. The hands, in spite of arthritic crooks and enlarged joints, were musician's hands, also like her mother's. Notes of Chopin tumbled through Leila's brain as when she was small and wanted to curl up inside the music, pressing her cheek to the side of the upright her mother played so flawlessly.

"I guess the crown was Big Nurse's idea?" Leila had asked, arranging the Christmas bouquet she had brought, blood red carnations spinning a web of gold stars.

"Fraulein demanded it," MamaLee said. "Law, if I have to sing 'Up on the Housetop, Click, Click, Click' one more time, shaking those little jingle bells like some kind of shriveled-up kindergartner, I'm going to tear off my clothes and run screaming naked down the halls. Nekkid."

And Leila had buried her head against the old woman's curved shoulder and sobbed for her mother's music and her father's laughter while MamaLee soothed, and Joe went to get her a cup of coffee.

for the ladies' room, or "Law, I cut my foot," when the neighbor's collie left a fecal lawn ornament for her Enna Jetticks to find. Now, her long recovery from hip replacement surgery in the wake of her daughter's passing had become a wait for her own passing.

A couple of years after her brother Coleman's death, Leila had grappled with the concept of heaven and the stars and infinity. It had been exasperating. Her finite mind fought to conjure the notion in a way she could visualize, but it seemed to her that all things had to end somewhere—way past the solar system, to be sure—beyond the Milky Way all swirled about like a Van Gogh, stars swelling and burning out at once. Her child's mind envisioned a wall—a dead end for the universe—with a sign on it: "Everything ends here. Sincerely, God." Yet walls had other sides to them, which, after all, made them walls. So her ten-year-old brain had conjectured that all of her own eternity lived within a shoebox sitting in another girl's closet, like her own, but bigger. And that girl's universe, too, was nestled in a shoebox in yet another, larger girl's closet, and—Leila had to give up on comprehending infinity. Instead, she latched on to the spiritual lacework of genealogy and ancestors whose souls led to hers and, years later, to her daughter's. "You are not about to catch the bus, MamaLee," she said again.

She had sipped the coffee Joe delivered and had become warmed as his fingers squeezed her shoulder. MamaLee was delighted with the miniature of Tia Maria he had brought her, sipping it daintily from a clear plastic hospital cup, fussing that she missed her nightly nip and her own sherry glasses. She had been leery of Joe in the beginning, had not understood him and his Philadelphia-Italian roots, suspicious of what that Yankee gene pool might do to the sturdy magnolia that was the Dulaney family tree. But now they were easy together, and MamaLee could bat her eyes, play the Rebel belle, and dish up double entendres. That day, five days back, they even seemed conspiratorial, exchanging more than a few furtive grins.

"I swan," MamaLee had said ages ago, upon learning of their engagement. "What kind of a name is 'D'Amico'? 'Leila D'Amico'—law, it sounds like a striptease artist." But she had been polite, Joe amused, toying with her edgy gentility over the years via invented Mafioso tales and inside jokes.

"You know, MamaLee," he would say. "I've got a buddy—Jimmy 'The Orange' Cappuccino—who'll take out Nurse Ratched for you. If you've got twenty grand, she'll sleep with the fishes."

"You mean cap her?" MamaLee said. "I'll give you, let's see . . ." she fished in her brassiere and counted out, "one, two, three, four—I'll give you four dollars. And she's not worth half that much."

And they would laugh some more and plot, Leila envying the grandmother's strength and humor in spite of being so alone in the world. Drowsing on Joe's strong shoulder as they drove home, Leila began to feel goldfishy nibbles of shame at the grief she held so close, having fended off joy all year, too often going numbly through a day, fuzzily aware of Trish and her tiny crises or the business she ran as though sleepwalking through a poppy field.

Once, several months earlier, Joe had hinted that MamaLee might be better off living with them, at least for a while, but Leila had dropped the glass of wine she was holding, covered her face with her hands and sobbed that she could not be the audience at yet another death. How could he even think, Leila had accused, that she could stand a drop more than she had been given when she barely functioned as it was? So he held her, wrapping the warm reassurance of the fiercest sun about her, and promised to keep the Reaper at bay.

She had breathed Joe's cologne, the soft wool of his sweater, and thought of something he had said to her when Trish was born: "It's going away, you know—this culture of yours, family trees and Southern sensibility. But if you need to hold on, I'll help you." And she had known that he would, just as he had borne her up when the days were disintegrating. She thought of something else as well: promises given with conviction to her mother, to MamaLee, and to Joe, and reciprocated back to her, that none of them was ever to be shut away in a nursing home, no matter how upscale and swanky the façade. The nibbles of guilt became voracious gulps, a vague anger struggling to confront her sadness. In spite of the family pact, MamaLee had not questioned where she was.

Now Leila sipped her Christmas sherry and fingered an ornament on the over-dressed tree, reflected light slipping through webs of pine needles. Santa is here, she decided, setting about the business of laying out Trish's toys. A soccer ball. A Candyland game. Malibu Barbie in her pink dune buggy, white blonde hair catching silver whispers of glows from the hissing fireplace. Glaring balls tinkling a brassy protest when Leila accidentally nudged the tree. Barbie's Dream House, a boxed replica of adult décor, entertainment, and excess—a little girl's grown-up fantasy world. The Nutcracker's Sugar Plum Fairy chimed her through the stocking preparation—walnuts and oranges in the toe, Wal-Mart trinkets to give shape, and, as always, one very special surprise, this year a necklace, a gold heart-shaped locket with pictures of Leila's parents inside, diamond chip stars on the outside. She was attentive to details, careful to leave Santa's snacks half-eaten, cake crumbs strewn about as though he ate hurriedly as he worked, milk glass drained, napkin wadded. All accomplished, she finished her sherry to the "Carol of the Bells" and the mantel clock chiming three times, finally mounting the stairs heavily, shoulders curved forward. Sleeping alone was not an option, and she crawled into bed with Trish, snuggling, holding her daughter spoon-like beneath MamaLee's comforter, the tiny body nestled against her as if still in the womb, surrounded by music and glow-in-the-dark stars.

Furtive metallic shards of a broken ornament glinted from beneath the barren tree. Odd abstracts of mangled boxes, wads of paper, stiff and sharp, and knots and curves of ribbon were strewn about the living room. They had attacked the gifts in a hedonistic frenzy, following Trish's lead, exclaiming over the thoughtfully chosen, giggling over the outrageously useless. Trish was rolling Barbie across the Oriental rug, a fit highway for the fluff of femininity in the hot pink vehicle, while Joe and Leila drank coffee, inventorying the loot. When Joe brought out yet another box for Leila to unwrap, she assumed it was his gift to her, looking at him quizzically when she found a pair of crystal vases shrouded in tissue paper.

"From MamaLee," he said.

"Yes, I know. They belonged to her mother. But. . ."

"She thinks you need more fresh flowers around here."

The funeral home image skipped behind Leila's eyes, the two closed caskets, blankets of roses, sprays and gardenia-laden vases overpowering the chapel, watercolor shapes, impressionistic petals, pistils, pristine loveliness that mocked the dead.

"That is," Joe went on, "I think you do. You used to keep us in free flowers all the time."

Trish giggled, danced over to her father and whispered to him. "Sure," he said to her. "It's grand finale time."

Leila narrowed her eyes. "You're very mysterious." He was a sucker for Christmas, she knew; over the years they had battled to outdo one another, but the once-spirited competition had become nonexistent for her, and regret tugged at her for letting him down.

"I have to warn you, I'm throwing down the gauntlet. We're

going to keep doing Christmas right," Joe said. "And by the way, I had to move your mother's piano."

"Joe!"

"It had to be. I needed the music room for your present and, well—two pianos? Come on. I put your mother's in storage for Trish. Or better yet, give it to the church."

"But when did you do it? How did you get it by me?" She was intrigued, letting the church comment go. He knew she could never part with her mother's piano.

Joe watched her for what seemed a long time, Trish tugging at his robe. "Don't you realize it's been nearly a year since you've been in that room, or even opened it? I could have a harem in there and you'd be clueless." He stood by the gauzily curtained French doors. "I've done quite a bit in there, actually."

"No, I didn't realize," Leila whispered, stunned, seeing what pains she had taken to avoid it, how enveloped she had been in grief, furiously sealed, like the chromosphere of an angry star.

"So who'll open the present?" Joe asked. "And you'd better like it. I waited for hours last night to bring it in. Got no sleep. Ask me how much sleep I got."

"Me! Me!" Trish squealed, pushing past her mother, flinging back the doors, racing to clamber up onto the spool bed, careful not to bump the old woman's feeble bones. "I kept the secret! MamaLee's going to catch the bus from here!" the little girl exclaimed. "Only she says the bus has a gazillion stops to make first!"

"Law, I thought y'all never would be through in there. All that ripping and tearing sounded like a herd of mules in a cornfield." MamaLee indicated a bucket holding champagne and sparkling grape juice for Trish. With a startling absence of anger, Leila at once noticed how the room was done over with MamaLee's very favorite keepsakes, photographs, and paintings. Her deceased husband's portrait hung over her bed. "All my suitors will just have to tolerate it," the old woman giggled and Leila felt herself smile from a reservoir of joy that had not been there an hour ago. A walker was beside the bed, a few special pieces of furniture arranged at cozy angles, and Joe was showing off his handiwork with a flourish.

"That little sofa folds down into a bed," he said, "in case we ever need any help to stay over. I had a handrail installed here . . ." he pointed to the adjoining bathroom. "Turns out this room is the perfect place." Joe ceased his tour and looked squarely at Leila. "Hope you're okay about the piano."

Leila nodded and held her husband's eyes. She was awed by the certainty she discovered in her grandmother's presence. She hugged a soft whisper of purplish hair to her cheek. "MamaLee. This is so right. And I am so ashamed. Why didn't we do this sooner? What was I thinking?"

"You weren't," Joe said. "Thinking, that is. But Trish was." He took the champagne bottle out of the bucket. "I didn't want to push anything on you. But now—it's just that Trish and I—well. Trish and I thought it would be a great idea. It turns out, so did

MamaLee. Of course she had to be sold on it. Actually, I even had to sell her house for her before she would begin to consider it. She wants the money to go toward her keep."

"You crazy old lady!" Leila smiled.

"It was me, Mama. I remembered the promise," Trish said. "And MamaLee said you wimped out. So I had the idea. But Daddy helped me plan everything."

"And I vow before all that is holy," the grandmother said to the popping of the cork, "that I will not offer advice, not enter your quarters without first knocking, follow the eleventh commandment that saith: 'Thou shalt mind thine own business' and keep both feet on the floor when being courted."

Champagne glasses tinkled finely as Joe poured, Trish lowering her nose to tickly grape juice bubbles. "But now here's the serious part of my speech," MamaLee said. "And it is this: I know that you're hurt, Little Leila, but for your hurting to take you from those who love you— it would be like another death." She stopped, looked at her hands twisting the fabric of her dressing gown. "I for one would be hard-pressed to bear it." Her voice trembled for a moment, eyes filling. She forced a little laugh. "No. I don't think we'll be entertaining Mr. Death for a right long piece." The grandmother brushed her ancient fingers through Trish's dark hair. "And P.S. If you decide it's too much on you, I'll go back to Nurse Hitler with not so much as a whimper. Joe stored all my things away with your mother's piano—for you or Trish or the

Goodwill. You know, sugar, it's only stuff—a bunch of clutter, all things considered."

They drank a toast to their new lives, and along with the sweet champagne, Leila drank in a sense of rightness, an unfamiliar serenity enfolding her like the velveteen petals of a perfect flower. She looked at MamaLee and shook her head so lightly that no one could have noticed. Here was this woman giving her comfort, from deep within the promise of her own twilight days, having borne with such grace the weight of having buried her only child along with unspoken good-byes. Leila touched her daughter's cheek and could not comprehend such a loss—it was as unthinkable as infinity, as overpowering as being accepted in her own self-absorbed sadness.

They would spend warm evenings honoring the ancestors long gone, and the lives so recently summoned to the heavens. Trish would relive the history and high times of MamaLee's bathtub gin-swilling, jazzed, and youthful days, while Joe would savor the security only a mother could give. Leila would learn from a life well-lived, of death put by, and sparkling instants of truth in mundane moments present. She would waltz as a child with the notes of her mother's music. She would bring penance with fresh flowers and find absolution in the stars.

CONTRIBUTORS

Glen Allison of Tupelo, Mississippi, is the author of the Al Forte mystery series set in New Orleans, as well as the biographical *Still Standing Tall,* the story of the Grammy-nominated Williams Brothers, published by Billboard Books. He has written for newspapers and magazines including *Guideposts, Memphis Magazine, Ford Magazine, Mississippi Magazine,* and others.

Rick Anderson is a native Mississippian who grew up in the Mississippi Delta, completed his undergraduate and graduate degrees at Delta State University, taught art for twenty-five years in public schools in Mississippi, and painted professionally, winning more than 150 awards in regional and national art shows and festivals. Anderson continues to create his art, and in 2003, his first children's book, *M is for Magnolia: A Mississippi Alphabet Book,* was published. Anderson has since had three other children's books published, with three more coming out in the fall of 2008. He resides in Clinton, Mississippi, with his wife, Merrie, a librarian at Clinton Junior High School. They have one son, Denman, an actor living in Washington, D. C.

Mary Ward Brown is a native of Alabama and the author of two collections of short stories, *Tongues of Flame* (1986) and *It Wasn't All Dancing* (2001). She received the PEN/Hemingway Award in 1987, the Lillian Smith Award in 1991, and the Harper Lee Award in 2002. She has completed a memoir that will be published by the University of Alabama Press in early 2009. Brown lives on the farm where she grew up, between Marion and Selma, Alabama.

Robert Olen Butler won the Pulitzer Prize for Fiction in 1993 for *A Good Scent from a Strange Mountain,* a collection of short stories about the Vietnamese diaspora in southern Louisiana. He is the author of ten novels and five books of short fiction. In addition to numerous other prizes, he has twice won a National Magazine Award in fiction. He is a professor of creative writing at Florida State University in Tallahassee, and his most recent book is a collection of short stories titled *Intercourse.*

Sheryl Cornett lives with her family in Chapel Hill, North Carolina, and teaches at North Carolina State University. After attending the American University in Paris, she graduated from Miami University (Ohio) and UNC-Chapel Hill. Her stories, poems, and essays have appeared in many journals and magazines, including *Mars Hill Review, Image, Pembroke Magazine, Raleigh News and Observer, Independent Weekly,* and others. She is revising her young-adult novel, *Mignonne,* and seeking a publisher for it. Her story "Luke" is part of a collection of linked stories called *What the Angel Said.*

Suzanne Hudson won the Hackney Literary Award and a $5,500 National Endowment for the Arts and Humanities prize, then withdrew from the publishing world for twenty-five years until the publication of *Opposable Thumbs,* a collection of short stories in 2001, followed soon after by a novel, *A Temple of Trees.* Hudson lives and teaches in south Alabama.

Charline R. McCord, a resident of Clinton, Mississippi, was born in Hattiesburg and grew up in Laurel, Mississippi, and Jackson, Tennessee. She holds a Ph.D. in English from the University of Southern Mississippi and bachelor's and master's degrees in English from Mississippi College, where she won the Bellamann Award for Creative Writing and edited the literary magazine. She has coedited a series of books with Judy H. Tucker: *Growing Up in Mississippi* (University Press of Mississippi, 2008), *A Dixie Christmas* (Algonquin, 2005), *Christmas in the South* (Algonquin, 2004), *A Very Southern Christmas* (Algonquin, 2003), and *Christmas Stories from Mississippi* (University Press of Mississippi, 2001).

Margaret McMullan is the author of four novels including *In My Mother's House* (Picador, 2003) and the young-adult novel *When I Crossed No-Bob* (Houghton Mifflin, 2007). Her work has appeared in *Glamour, Chicago Tribune, Southern Accents, TriQuarterly, Michigan Quarterly Review, The Southern Quarterly Anthology, Other Voices, Boulevard, Ploughshares,* and *The Sun,* among others. From Newton, Mississippi, McMullan received her master's of fine arts degree in fiction from the University of Arkansas, Fayetteville. She is currently a professor of English at the University of Evansville, in Evansville, Indiana, where she is working on a collection of short stories and two new novels for Houghton Mifflin.

Mark Richard was born in Lake Charles, Louisiana, and grew up in Texas and Virginia. He is the author of the best-selling novel *Fishboy* and two short-story collections, *Charity* and *Ice at the Bottom of the World,* for which he won the PEN/Ernest Hemingway Award. He now lives in Los Angeles.

Kay Sloan, a native of Mississippi, is the author of two novels, *Worry Beads* and *The Patron Saint of Red Chevys,* chosen as a "Discover Great Writers" book by Barnes and Noble. Her poetry and essays have appeared in many journals and magazines, and her film documentary, *Suffragettes in the Silent Cinema,* has been shown at film festivals throughout Europe and America. She is also the author of three books on American history. Sloan resides in southern Ohio, where she is a professor at Miami University.

Elizabeth Spencer, a native of Carrollton, Mississippi, received a master of arts degree from Vanderbilt. Since 1948, she has published nine novels, seven short-story collections, a memoir, and a dramatic play. A Broadway adaptation of her novel *Light in the Piazza* won six Tony Awards. After an extensive stay in Italy, Spencer came home to teach writing at the University of North Carolina until 1992. Her honors include five O. Henry Awards; the Governor's Award for Achievement in Literature from the Mississippi Arts Commission, 2006; the PEN/Malamud Award for Short Fiction, 2007; the Award of Merit from the American Academy of Arts and Letters; a Guggenheim Fellowship, and many others.

Judy H. Tucker, a native Mississippian, lives in Jackson. In 2007 she was the recipient of a Mississippi Arts Commission Literary Fellowship. She has edited five anthologies with coeditor Charline R. McCord and two short-story collections with coeditor Lottie Boggan. Her plays have been produced and/or read at New Stage and Fondren Workshop Theatre in Jackson and the Alabama Shakespeare Festival.

Olympia Vernon is the author of three critically acclaimed novels. Her first, *Eden,* was nominated for the Pulitzer Prize and won the 2004 American Academy of Arts and Letters Richard and Linda Rosenthal Foundation Award. *Eden* was also a *New York Times* "New and Notable Book." Her second novel, *Logic,* was nominated for the Mississippi Institute of Arts and Letters Award. *A Killing in This Town,* published in 2006, was a *New York Times* "Editors Choice Pick" and the winner of the first annual Ernest J. Gaines Award for Literary Excellence. Vernon is also the winner of the 2005 Louisiana Governor's Award for Professional Artist of the Year and is currently the Hallie Brown Ford Chair at Willamette University.

Jacqueline F. Wheelock, born and reared on the Mississippi Gulf Coast, received bachelor of science and master of education degrees in English from Southern University in Baton Rouge, Louisiana, and a master of library science degree from the University of Southern Mississippi in Hattiesburg. In 2000, she won the Zora Neale Hurston-Bessie Head Fiction Award at the Gwendolyn Brooks Writers' Conference for "The Chifforobe," which appears in *From the Sleeping Porch* (2006). Her story "Christmas Lights," appears in *Christmas Stories from Mississippi* (University Press of Mississippi, 2001). In 2001 and 2003, her work placed in the William Faulkner Award for Short Fiction.

Ruth C. Williams is the coauthor of the widely acclaimed nonfiction book *Younger Than That Now—A Shared Passage from the Sixties* (Bantam/Random House, 2000). Williams won the Mississippi Institute of Arts and Letters Nonfiction Award in 2000, the Mississippi Library Association's Non-Fiction Award in 2003, and the Mississippi Library Association's Nonfiction Writer of the Year Award for 2003. Williams grew up in Yazoo City, attended Mary Baldwin College as a National Merit Scholar, and received a bachelor of fine arts degree from the University of Tennessee. Williams is a newspaper columnist, book reviewer, and technical writer. She lives in Flora, Mississippi, where she and her husband own and operate an advertising agency.

ACKNOWLEDGMENTS

Christmas is a time for giving, yes, but it's also a time to reflect and take inventory of the gifts we've already wrangled throughout the year, check to see if there's even a tiny corner left where we might stockpile something new and shiny, maybe break out the fruitcake and eggnog, and offer up a few heartfelt "thank yous" to fellow elves who worked behind the scenes to help make our lives jolly and bright. We wish to thank publisher Milburn Calhoun for inviting us into the Pelican fold this holiday season, editor in chief Nina Kooij for keeping us on track with this manuscript, and all the other good folks at Pelican whom we haven't actually glimpsed, but we share a Santa-like belief in because…well, because we're sharp enough to see the evidence of their magical handiwork on this project.

To the writers in this collection we sing all four stanzas of "Joy to the World," for that is what writers of stories are to us—a joy to the world! Thank you for sharing your special gifts with us this Christmas. We are grateful for your presence and presents in this book. And thanks tied with a big red bow to our talented illustrator Rick Anderson, who came through with good tidings of great joy after we called him up and crooned the duet, "We need a little Christmas—right this very minute!" For the lovely foreword to this collection, we offer Elizabeth Spencer a long-awaited Christmas snow and a bevy of muses bearing harps of gold and all caroling "O Little Town of Bethlehem."

We wish to bestow sparkly garlands of gratitude on our good friends Craig Gill and Carolyn Haines for their great wisdom and generosity in all things book related. Doyce Tucker is due a solid gold holiday star for his ongoing support, which allows Judy to do the things she loves (sitting behind a computer), and for not complaining about the worst meals in the world. And, if goodness is no longer a prerequisite, Santa might fly over and jettison a new tackle box and some blingy new bass baits for Bob McCord, who only mentioned a few hundred times that a certain person ought to stop working eighteen hours a day and maybe think about exercising and for quoting once and once only the scripture found in Proverbs 21:9. To John Tucker we give a complete "Hallelujah" chorus for his advice about all things grammatical; he is the best spell checker and fact checker around, and his editorial advice is always dead on. Finally, a festive Christmas bandanna gets tied on Gracie, the miniature schnauzer who lies in a mangerlike bed beneath the partner's desk, keeping her watch by night as miracles are undertaken on paper overhead—all in the hope of somehow making heaven and nature sing.

COPYRIGHT ACKNOWLEDGMENTS